STAGE EIGHT

STAGE EIGHT

One-act Plays

VIRGINIA BRADLEY

DODD, MEAD & COMPANY

NEW YORK

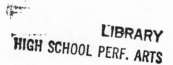

To Betty Myers
My sister, who believed in me
And to Howard Myers
More brother than brother-in-law

If these plays are not given for profit, they may be used for live performances without permission. For profit-making productions, permission must be obtained from the publisher.

2 3 4 5 6 7 8 9 10

Library of Congress Cataloging in Publication Data
Bradley, Virginia, date
    Stage eight.
    CONTENTS: The carousel and a cold fried egg.—
Nothing will rattle a regnant soul.—The bracelet
engagement.—[etc.]
    1. Children's plays. [1. One-act plays. 2. Plays]
I. Title.
PN6120.A5B6569   812'.041   77-6485
ISBN 0-396-07477-4

CONTENTS

THE CAROUSEL AND
A COLD FRIED EGG

SUMMARY

When Letty Simms is finally relieved of the obligation of caring for her invalid pa, she unexpectedly rejects her patient suitor, the pig farmer Lucius McNeil. "I can do what I like now," she tells him. And doing what she likes means a trip to the county fair to recapture the carefree days of her childhood and specifically the magic of the merry-go-round.

At the fairgrounds, Letty is eyed with concern by Lucius who has, of course, followed her, and eyed with envy by Clara Jane, a rational little girl who is encumbered by a cold egg sandwich and the weighty responsibility of "doing the right thing."

When the Ferris wheel locks its gears, excitement rises to a peak and Lucius rises to the emergency. Both Letty and Clara Jane make decisions which are difficult but definitely their own.

THE CAROUSEL AND A COLD FRIED EGG

CHARACTERS

LETTY SIMMS, A SPRIGHTLY YOUNG COUNTRY WOMAN WITH
    DREAMS

LUCIUS MC NEIL, LETTY'S PATIENT SUITOR AND A PROUD
    PIG FARMER

HOD TUCKER, ALSO A FARMER, SIMPLE BUT SINCERE

HENRIETTA TUCKER, HOD'S DOMINEERING WIFE

CLARA JANE, A LITTLE GIRL WITH A SANDWICH PROBLEM

CLARA JANE'S MOTHER

THE BARKER AT THE HOUSE OF THRILLS

THE MANAGER OF THE MIDWAY AT THE COUNTY FAIR

THE STRECHER BEARERS

THE COUNTY FAIR GUARD

THE MECHANIC

THE FAIR-GOING CROWD, AS MANY PEOPLE AS DESIRED

THE TIME: *A warm July evening in an earlier day*

SCENE ONE: *In front of Letty Simms's farmhouse. The
porch at stage left is the only important part of the set.
Whether or not there is anything done to suggest a yard
(flowers, a fence) is optional. There are two or three steps
to the porch, where there is an old-fashioned rocker. The
left exit is the door into the house.*

As the curtain opens LETTY *is rocking and singing. Each
time she goes backward her feet are lifted from the floor
making her seem almost like a child.* LUCIUS *enters from
the right, takes off his hat, wipes the sweat from his fore-*

head, and drops down on the steps. LETTY *does not stop rocking.*

LUCIUS. Well, your pa's gone, Letty. Dead and buried these three months now. We can set the day.

LETTY. (*stops rocking*) I'm not gonna marry you, Lucius.

LUCIUS. (*in surprise*) We been waiting six years, Letty. You needed to tend your pa, sick like he was, I know that. But there's nothing to stop us now.

LETTY. I'm to stop us.

LUCIUS. You think it's still too soon. I'll wait longer if you say so. But three months of grieving oughta satisfy anybody.

LETTY. Nothing to do with the time. It just come to me up there on the hill at pa's funeral, I got no one to worry about now but myself. I kinda like the idea.

LUCIUS. You mean you're just going to stay on here alone? You can't be thinking of that.

LETTY. No, I'm not thinking of that. I'm going to David City.

LUCIUS. David City! Letty, that makes no sense at all. You need somebody to look out for you.

LETTY. Lucius McNeil. After all the time I been caring for pa and this old farm you talk like I can't care for myself.

LUCIUS. You got to admit, Letty, you've not been doing very smart things lately. First off you sold all your pa's pigs. Then you give away the only horse you had on the place. And now this talk about David City.

LETTY. It's not talk.

LUCIUS. You got no folks there.

LETTY. I do so. Have you clean forgot my cousin Emmeline Potts? I'll visit a spell with her, and then after I sell the farm I'll just find a little place of my own. But that's not what's important right now. Tomorrow's the last day of the County Fair at David City, and that's where I'm going—even before I call Emmeline.

LUCIUS. I don't understand you, Letty.

LETTY. Well, I'm a grown woman. I can do what I like. (*She gets a dreamy look on her face.*) I only been to the fair once. Pa took me when I was seven. And last night I dreamed about the merry-go-round.

LUCIUS. The merry-go-round!

LETTY. (*gets up from her rocker and comes down the steps past* LUCIUS *to center stage*) A merry-go-round's pure magic, Lucius. The music's like no other music in the world. And sitting atop one of those fine painted horses . . . (*She pantomimes the movement of the carousel and her voice gets mellow.*) Why, you feel like you could go anyplace you've a mind to. I've got a hankering to see if the magic's still there. (*She pauses in her charade.*)

LUCIUS. Magic's pulling rabbits out of a hat, Letty. Something's happened to you. You never been like this before. And you said it. You're a grown woman. Merry-go-rounds is for kids.

LETTY. No use to argue. I'm going to the fair. (*She resumes her pantomime of the ride.*)

LUCIUS. (*his thoughts still on the merry-go-round*) I don't see nothing good in going around like that anyhow. And I wish you'd sit down, Letty. It makes my head spin just to watch you. When I was fifteen I got me caught up on the Dutch windmill in the south pasture, and I like to died. (*He holds his head in recollection.*)

LETTY. (*stops her movement but does not sit*) Then you've got no feel for what I'm talking about. Besides there's more. I'm going to ride the Ferris wheel. Pa wouldn't let me do that. He said nobody oughta get that far off the ground.

LUCIUS. (*gets up and moves toward* LETTY *at center stage*) If it's the fair you want, Letty, I reckon I could take you. I wasn't planning on it this year, but gosh, I wouldn't mind seeing the pigs.

LETTY. Pigs! I guess that's part of it. I don't think I ever want to be in pigs again.

LUCIUS. 'Tain't just pigs, Letty. Mine's good stock.

LETTY. You didn't come here to talk stock, Lucius. And there's no need to trouble yourself. (*She crosses to the porch, then turns.*) Hod and Henrietta Tucker are going in to the fair tomorrow to pick up a young bull, and they said I could ride along.

LUCIUS. (*Suddenly angry, he grabs hold of Letty's wrist.*) You can't go, Letty. I won't let you.

LETTY. (*lifts his hand from her arm*) You got no say in the matter. I guess I did reckon we'd be wed when pa died, but you got no rope around my neck. Now if you aim to take on so you best get yourself out of my yard —off my property. I'm going to bed. I got me a big day tomorrow. (*She sweeps up the steps and into the house. During this action* HOD *enters quietly from the right.*)

HOD. I coulda told you you was wasting your time, Luke.

LUCIUS. (*turns to* HOD, *startled*) Hod Tucker, you scared me half to death. What you doing? Following me?

HOD. I ain't following you, Luke. I just come to tell Letty we was fixing to start in the morning 'bout six. (*shouts past* LUCIUS *into the house*) Hear that, Letty? 'Bout six.

LUCIUS. Fine friend you are.

HOD. Doggone it, Luke. I'm on your side.

LUCIUS. Don't look like it none. Taking Letty off to David City.

HOD. It ain't me. It's Henrietta. She says Letty's been struck mighty hard what with never knowing her ma and her pa ailing all them years.

LUCIUS. But why can't she stay to home?

HOD. It don't make no sense to me neither, Luke.

LUCIUS. Well, one thing sure. Somebody got to see to it Letty gives up this fool idea, and with Henrietta working against me, you're not gonna be any help. Deke Olson can tend my pigs tomorrow, and I'll go to the fair too. I can get on the road by seven. You'll have a head start, but you won't make much time in that broken down truck of yours.

HOD. You ain't mad at me, are you, Luke?

LUCIUS. Nah. You can't be blamed for Henrietta.

LETTY. (*calls from the house*) Will you two do your wagging someplace else?

HOD. I'm going.

LETTY. Well, get along then. Goodness knows, a body that's going to the fair at six in the morning needs a mite a sleep. (*She starts her singing again.*)

HOD. I'm glad you ain't mad at me, Luke. (*He exits right and* LUCIUS *drops back onto the porch steps again with his head in his hands as the curtain falls.*)

SCENE TWO: *A clearing in the middle of the fairgrounds. Downstage left is an exit leading to the home exhibits and downstage right one which leads to the livestock pens. There are signs to direct the crowds. The upstage exits go off to the midway rides, right to the merry-go-round and left to the Ferris wheel. Although these attractions cannot be seen by the audience, they can be seen by the characters on stage. The Ferris wheel, as a matter of fact, is just beyond the exit. At the back is the curtained entrance to the House of Thrills and close beside it the curtained exit. Between them is the ticket stand for that concession and a straight wooden chair. There is a bench at right center with a trash can beside it.*

As the curtain opens it is still early in the day. The BARKER *for the House of Thrills is seated in the chair which is tipped back at a precarious angle. His straw hat is down over his eyes and he is dozing.* CLARA JANE *and her* MOTHER *enter from downstage right.* CLARA JANE *is hugging a box of caramel corn and her* MOTHER *carries an old-fashioned round tin lunch pail. They come all the way to center stage and the* MOTHER *looks appraisingly around the area. Finally she directs* CLARA JANE *to the bench.*

MOTHER. This spot will do, Clara Jane. I don't see, though, why you couldn't stay with your papa and me.

CLARA JANE. It smells bad down there. (*She holds her nose.*)

MOTHER. Chickens and cows are your papa's business. Fine farmer's daughter you make. But as long as he said it was all right for you to wait here, I guess it is. Just mind you don't stray or we'd never find you when the crowd comes in.

CLARA JANE. Can I ride on the Ferris wheel?

MOTHER. Land sakes no. Nobody should get that far off the ground.

CLARA JANE. The merry-go-round, then?

MOTHER. Didn't you hear me, Clara Jane? I don't want you wandering around by yourself.

CLARA JANE. Could you take me on the merry-go-round before you go back to the chickens, Mama?

MOTHER. Goodness, child, I got no time for that kind of foolishness. I'm going around in circles enough as it is without getting on those silly horses. Now here's your lunch. (*She gives* CLARA JANE *the lunch pail, then goes to the* BARKER *who is still dozing.*) Mister. (*She shakes him.*) Mister.

BARKER. (*waking up with a start and almost losing his balance on the chair*) Hey, lady. Don't do that.

MOTHER. Excuse me, mister, but will you just keep an eye on the little girl here for awhile? If you're not too busy. She won't give you any trouble.

BARKER. I'll keep an eye on her all right. Don't you worry none.

(*A* MECHANIC *in overalls and carrying a toolbox enters from upstage right, crosses to upstage left and exits.*)

CLARA JANE. (*opening her lunch*) What did you put in here, Mama?

MOTHER. It's a good lunch, Clara Jane, and mind you don't touch that caramel corn your papa bought you until your sandwich is gone. Understand?

CLARA JANE. It's not a egg sandwich is it, Mama? (*She makes a face.*) Not a egg.

MOTHER. There's nothing better than a good fried egg sandwich, and it's not to be wasted. Someplace in this world there's an orphan child who is starving. She'd be very happy to have that sandwich. You just remember that.

(*As Clara Jane's* MOTHER *heads for the downstage right exit* CLARA JANE *swings around on the bench to watch her.*)

CLARA JANE. I'll remember.

(*When her* MOTHER *exits,* CLARA JANE *turns back to face center stage, pulls a banana from the lunch pail, and starts to eat as* HENRIETTA *and* LETTY *enter from downstage left.*)

BARKER. (*seeing the potential customers, gets up from his chair and starts his patter*) OK ladies, put a little sparkle into your day . . .

LETTY. (*to the* BARKER) Not just now, mister. But I'll get around to it before I'm through.

(*The* BARKER *shrugs and goes back to his chair, putting his hat back over his eyes as it was.*)

HENRIETTA. Letty Simms. I still ain't got over you having gumption enough to come off here on your own.

LETTY. To tell the truth, Henrietta, I can't get over it myself. (*She looks off toward the merry-go-round.*) There it is. The merry-go-round. There it is. (*She is very excited.*)

HENRIETTA. You ain't been known for sticking up for your rights. Tied to your pa and that pig farm all these years.

LETTY. (*Still looking offstage toward the merry-go-round, she talks over her shoulder.*) Didn't have much choice about that.

HENRIETTA. Fiddlesticks. Your pa coulda hired Granny Perkins to tend him and let you have a little freedom.

LETTY. (*turns back to* HENRIETTA) I'm shut of that now, Henrietta. I just hope I'm not doing the wrong thing here though.

HENRIETTA. You hush that kind of talk. You don't know how lucky you are, Letty Simms, able to do just what you've a mind to. Sometimes I wish . . . (*She sighs.*) If I was to do it over I don't think I'd hitch up to Hod.

LETTY. (*with impatience*) Hod's a good man.

HENRIETTA. Oh, he's all right, I guess. But he's got no push and not much practical sense neither.

LETTY. (*anxious to cut off this conversation*) Sure you don't want to go on the merry-go-round with me? Just once, maybe?

HENRIETTA. It ain't that I wouldn't like to, Letty, but we wasn't counting on this as no pleasure trip. I do want to go back there (*She indicates the exit to the home exhibits from which they came.*) and pick up that quilt pattern and take a quick look at the bake booth. Then I'll swing on around to the barns again. Can't waste much time getting back to Hod. No telling what he'll do if I ain't there holding his hand. We might end up with a nanny goat 'stead of a bull. It don't seem right for me to leave you though.

LETTY. I don't mind, Henrietta, and I'm wanting to get on with my day. I've got it all planned out. First I'm riding the merry-go-round, then I'll go through this here House of Thrills, and then to the Ferris wheel. After that maybe I'll start over again.

HENRIETTA. Well, you have yourself a real good time, Letty. Don't forget your suitcase is waiting at the front gate, and you call Emmeline right away now.

> (*During these last speeches* CLARA JANE *has finished her banana, taken a fruit jar of milk out of her pail and finished that too.* HENRIETTA *exits downstage left and* LETTY *exits to the merry-go-round upstage right.*)
> (CLARA JANE, *pail in one hand, caramel corn in the other, follows* LETTY *to the exit and then turns to the* BARKER.)

CLARA JANE. Did you hear that? She's a grown lady and she's going on the merry-go-round. Gollies. (*The* BARKER *does not move and pays no attention to her.*) Say, you're not keeping a eye on me, mister. But that's all right. You really don't have to. Like mama said I won't give any trouble. When my mama says "stay put" I stay put. (*She looks toward the merry-go-round again.*) I sure do wish I could go with that lady with the rose on her hat though. (*turns back to the* BARKER) I sure would like some of this caramel corn too. Say, you wouldn't want a egg sandwich would you?

BARKER. (*lifts his straw hat from his face*) Your mama said you had to eat that.

CLARA JANE. No, she didn't. She just said it had to be gone.

(HOD *and* LUCIUS *enter from downstage right and the* BARKER *sees possible customers.*)

BARKER. Don't bother me now, little girl. I'm busy. (*He gets up and starts his spiel.*) OK fellas, take a little time to enjoy yourselves. (HOD *and* LUCIUS *ignore him.*)

HOD. You musta burned up the road, Luke. We ain't hardly been here long enough to spit. You think you can find Letty? Henrietta said they was going to the front gate.

LUCIUS. I'll find her.

BARKER. (*continues talking*) Step right this way. The House of Thrills. Don't miss it. Watch the little ladies in there ahanging onto their skirts . . . Ooo-Woo.

CLARA JANE. (*to* BARKER) There isn't anybody in there yet and you know it. (*The* BARKER *gives* CLARA JANE *a dirty look and since he is being ignored he gives up and goes back to his stand.*)

LUCIUS. (*to* CLARA JANE) Little girl, you seen a lady 'bout so high (*he indicates Letty's height*) with a round, flat hat and a rose sticking up on it?

CLARA JANE. Sure I seen her. She was mighty anxious to get to the merry-go-round. The other lady headed off that way. (*She points off toward the home exhibits exit.*)

But the one with the rose . . . gollies, she'd make a good mama.

HOD. I gotta catch up with Henrietta 'fore she heads back to the barns. I can't find no bull down there marked "Tucker" and Henrietta's gonna be hopping mad. Good luck, Luke.

LUCIUS. Thanks, Hod, I'll need it. (*turns to* CLARA JANE *as* HOD *exits downstage left to follow* HENRIETTA) The merry-go-round this way?

CLARA JANE. Sure, mister. You can see it. (*She points off toward the merry-go-round upstage right.*) You can even see the lady with the rose. There she is on that pretty black horse. Gollies, is she your lady, mister? (LUCIUS *tries to spot* LETTY.) Are you gonna ride too?

LUCIUS. Looks like I'm gonna have to. (LUCIUS *exits right to the merry-go-round. The* MANAGER *enters from upstage left with the* MECHANIC *on his heels.*)

MECHANIC. I'm telling you, Mr. Becker, that motor needs more than a screwdriver and a squirt of oil. You take my word for it.

MANAGER. It'll be all right. Let me do the worrying. It's the last day anyhow.

(*As the* MANAGER *and the* MECHANIC *exit downstage right, a few stragglers enter upstage right and the* BARKER *starts his pitch.*)

BARKER. Right through the curtain here, folks. A barrel of thrills and chills and spine tingling adventure. I don't want to give anything away, fellas, but the girls'll be hanging on to you for dear life.

(*During this action and dialogue* CLARA JANE, *still clutching her pail and caramel corn, wanders around the clearing. She does a hopscotch step, looks off toward the Ferris wheel and, when the customers buy tickets and enter the House of Thrills, she comes back to the* BARKER.)

CLARA JANE. I never been in a thrill house. What's in there?

BARKER. If I told you you wouldn't come in to find out, now would you?

CLARA JANE. I won't anyhow. Mama wouldn't allow me. So you might just as well tell me what's in there.

BARKER. All kinds of terrifying things, little girl. You'd be scared.

CLARA JANE. I would not. I'm not scared of anything. It's mama's scared. (*She peeks through the curtained exit of the House of Thrills.*) I can see the barrel though.

BARKER. C'mon now, get away from the exit. Don't be in the way of the paying customers.

CLARA JANE. We had a rolling barrel like that at the car-

nival at Stopes Corner last year. I know about that barrel. Do folks have to walk through it before they can
get out, mister?

BARKER. You said it, little girl. If they can.

> (*A few more customers enter from downstage left,
> the* BARKER *goes into his pitch and* CLARA JANE
> *wanders back to the bench.*)

BARKER. Here you go, folks. Have the time of your lives.
Get your tickets and go right through the curtain here.
Surprises galore and more and more. Biggest bargain on
the midway. Take as long as you like and as long as you
can take it. There's plenty of excitement, folks, and all
the thrills you could ask for. (*The customers walk on
by as he talks and* LUCIUS *enters on wobbly legs from
upstage right. He has gone one round on the carousel
and has had to get off.*)

CLARA JANE. You didn't stay on the merry-go-round very
long, mister. (*She gets up from the bench and looks off
to the merry-go-round.*) The lady with the rose is still
riding. She sure likes it. *Is* she your lady?

LUCIUS. (*sits on the bench and holds his head, groaning*)
Are you lost, little girl?

CLARA JANE. Course I'm not lost. I'm just supposed to stay
here till mama comes back after me. She's down at the

chickens with papa. Papa's been here to the fair all week. He brought in a brown cow and just thousands of chickens. Mama and me stayed home. Somebody had to. But today's the last day and mama's down there helping papa clean up so's tonight when the fair closes we can pack up and get for home. (*She pauses to look at* LUCIUS.) You sure look green, mister. Would you like my sandwich. (*She takes the sandwich out of the pail and opens up the wrapping.*) I hate egg sandwiches. Mama never fries 'em hard enough and the yellow's all runny. Look. (*She shows* LUCIUS.) Yuck! (LUCIUS *holds his stomach and turns away.*) I don't blame you, mister. How about some caramel corn? It'd be all right for *you* to have some. (LUCIUS *puts one hand over his mouth and covers his eyes with the other as* LETTY *hurries in from the merry-go-round, buys a ticket to the House of Thrills and enters through the curtain.*)

CLARA JANE. (*who has seen her*) Hey, there's the rose lady. She went right smack into the thrill house. Gollies!

LUCIUS. (*managing to get to his feet*) In here? (*He starts to go after* LETTY.) Wait, Letty, wait. I want to talk to you. (*He exits into the thrill house.*)

BARKER. Hey, fella, you can't go in there without a ticket. (*He follows* LUCIUS *through the curtain as* HENRIETTA *hurries in from downstage right.*)

HENRIETTA. (*breathlessly*) Little girl, you see a man 'bout so tall (*She indicates Hod's height.*) with a checkered shirt and a big old cowboy hat and looked like he was lost?

CLARA JANE. I know who you're looking for, lady. He was with that other man who was looking for the lady with the rose. That man found out she was on the merry-go-round, but then she got off and went in there and he followed her.

HENRIETTA. In here, you say? (*She heads for the House of Thrills.*)

CLARA JANE. No, wait! That was the other one. The one you're looking for went that way hunting for you. (*She points off toward the home exhibits.*) He was in a awful hurry too. Are you hopping mad?

HENRIETTA. (*sighs and comes to sit on the bench beside* CLARA JANE) That Hod Tucker will be the death of me. We ain't gonna get home till midnight at this rate.

(*The* MECHANIC *enters downstage right, crosses to upstage left and exits.*)

CLARA JANE. (*to* HENRIETTA) Say, I couldn't interest you in a egg sandwich, could I? It's a little runny, but there's nothing better than a egg sandwich. That's what mama says.

HENRIETTA. I wouldn't think of taking your lunch. But I'm sure your mama makes good sandwiches.

CLARA JANE. Just if you don't have to eat them. Mama keeps telling me about this orphan child who'd be happy to have my sandwiches. All I say is just point her to me. She can have this one and welcome to it.

HENRIETTA. (*who has not been listening but has been fanning herself with her handkerchief*) Well, now that I've caught my breath . . . (*She gets up.*) You say the man I'm looking for went off this way? (CLARA JANE *nods and as* HENRIETTA *exits downstage left* LETTY *comes out of the House of Thrills.*)

CLARA JANE. (*to* LETTY) Hey, lady . . . lady . . .

LETTY. (*who was about to take off for the Ferris wheel*) Yes?

CLARA JANE. I'd sure like to talk to you.

LETTY. I guess 'twon't hurt to sit a bit. Though I've a lot more to do.

CLARA JANE. You're having a whole bucket of fun aren't you? Did you like the thrill house? The man wouldn't tell me nothing about it. Was it good and scary?

LETTY. (*Seeing* CLARA JANE *as she herself was as a child,* LETTY *dramatizes the secrets of the House of Thrills, exaggerating the terrors for Clara Jane's benefit.*) Well, I should just say it was. Yessiree. First off there was this whooshing wind. I had to hang on to my hat—

and my skirt too. And then there was the mirrors. Oh, law, the mirrors. I was fat and then thin and then tall and then squat. And finally so small I warn't hardly there. The next place was dark, black as the middle of the coal pile. All I could see was eyes, bright, staring eyes, and things poked out of the dark to touch me, and there was a crazy laughing—screams too—and then all of a sudden, wham, bang bingo, the floor just disappeared and down I went on a kind of chute, bouncing and jostling along until I slid out onto something soft and feathery. It was still pretty dark, and I couldn't find any way out. Then all at once I saw it . . .

CLARA JANE. (*who has been enjoying the excitement*) I know—the barrel. Where you going now?

LETTY. Ferris wheel's next. Would you like to go on the Ferris wheel?

CLARA JANE. Oh, gollies, would I ever. But I can't.

LETTY. I know. (*with a smile of understanding*) Your pa won't let you.

CLARA JANE. Not papa. Mama's the one. Besides I got to stay put. Right here. I always got to do what mama says.

LETTY. Well, you won't be sorry for that, honey. (*sighs*) No, you won't ever be sorry for that.

CLARA JANE. It's hard sometimes. (*She touches the lunch pail.*)

LETTY. (*thoughtfully*) Well, the thing is you just have to try to do what's right. Sometimes you have to decide things for yourself and that's harder.

CLARA JANE. Gollies, you sure *would* make a good mama.

LETTY. That's a nice thing to say, honey. A real nice thing to say.

CLARA JANE. And you know something else. I bet you'd have fun no matter what.

LETTY. (*gets up*) Well, I aim to try, but if I don't move I'll never pack in all the fun I got stacked up for to-day. Good-bye now. Maybe when your mama comes back you can ride on the merry-go-round.

CLARA JANE. Bye. (*She waves to* LETTY *who exits to the Ferris wheel as* HOD *enters downstage left.*)

HOD. Have you seen her? The lady with the lady with the rose?

CLARA JANE. Gollies, you people are all lost. And mama worries about me. Sure I seen her. She was here looking for you. It's easier to keep track of the rose lady. And she's the only one not looking for anybody.

(LUCIUS *crawls out of the House of Thrills exit.*
He is dazed and unable to get off the ground.)

HOD. Luke! You look awful. Did you find Letty?

LUCIUS. I found her all right. I just can't catch up with
her.

CLARA JANE. She came out of the thrill house. Off to the
Ferris wheel now.

LUCIUS. That dad-blamed barrel.

(*At that moment the* BARKER *crawls out of the*
House of Thrills.)

CLARA JANE. Don't nobody besides the rose lady know
how to get through that barrel without falling down.
All you have to do is keep walking to the side with
the roll. And you just prance out like nothing. (*She*
pantomimes the action.) See, it's easy. (*No one pays*
any attention to her.)

BARKER. (*getting to his feet and collaring* LUCIUS) You
can't get away with not buying a ticket, fella. OK, fork
over your two bits.

HOD. Give me a quarter, Luke.

(LUCIUS *gropes in his pocket for a coin which* HOD
hands to the BARKER. *As the* BARKER *goes back to*

his stand, HOD *helps* LUCIUS *to his feet and over to the bench.*)

LUCIUS. It's no use, Hod. I'm gonna give up. I guess I belong with the pigs—only things I'm to home with around here.

HOD. Well, I can't catch up with Henrietta neither. I been all over. I ain't even had time for nothing to eat.

CLARA JANE. (*perks up at this and gets her lunch pail*) Hey, mister, I bet you'd like to have this here sandwich. Mama says a egg . . . (CLARA JANE, *remembering her conversation with* LETTY, *cuts off her sentence and turns aside with a worried look.*)

HOD. Egg sandwiches is just about my favorite, little girl.

CLARA JANE. (*almost to herself*) Darn it. I suppose this is one of those deciding times.

HOD. What's the matter?

CLARA JANE. It's just now I'm not sure I can give it to you. I think the rose lady squashed the whole idea.

HOD. I don't know what you're talking about, but you got my tongue hanging out for an egg sandwich. I'm starving.

CLARA JANE. (*brightening*) Starving! Mister, I'm not even

gonna ask if you're a orphan. Starving is starving. Even mama'd see that. Here you are. (*She gives him the sandwich which he eats as he and* LUCIUS *exit downstage left.* CLARA JANE *turns to the* BARKER.) You heard him. He was starving.

MECHANIC'S VOICE OFFSTAGE. Get the manager. Get Mr. Becker.

BARKER. (*looks offstage*) Looks like trouble at the Ferris wheel. (*A few people drift out of the House of Thrills as the* MECHANIC *enters running from upstage left. He speaks to one of the customers.*)

MECHANIC. Tell them over at the entrance to call the fire department. The dang thing's stuck. I told Becker it needed more than a screwdriver. (*Someone exits downstage right to do as he asks.*)

CLARA JANE. (*looks offstage*) It's stuck all right and there's people way at the top. (*She spots* LETTY.) There's the rose lady, sure enough.

MECHANIC. Out of my way, little girl. (*Exits to Ferris wheel as the crowd begins to gather. Clara Jane's* MOTHER *enters downstage right.*)

MOTHER. What's going on?

CLARA JANE. The Ferris wheel's stuck, Mama.

(MANAGER *runs in from downstage right with a* GUARD *in a uniform.*)

MANAGER. Stand back now, folks. Stand back. We'll have things shipshape in no time. Just stay out of the way. (*Exits to the Ferris wheel. The* GUARD *stays behind and puts up a rope barrier to hold back the crowd.*)

MOTHER. And you wanted to get on that thing, Clara Jane. I told you it was dangerous. Well, I just hope they don't have to stay up there all night.

(HOD *and* HENRIETTA *and* LUCIUS *enter from downstage right.*)

CLARA JANE. You're missing all the excitement. Say mister, you know your lady's up there.

LUCIUS. She's what?

CLARA JANE. She's up there—way at the top. You can see her rose.

LUCIUS. Blamed contraption. Nobody in his right mind would get on that thing. (*He starts to climb over the rope and the* GUARD *pulls him back.*)

GUARD. You just stand back of the rope, buddy. There's enough trouble without you.

LUCIUS. How long she been up there?

GUARD. I don't know, fella. Just stand back.

MANAGER'S VOICE OFFSTAGE. No need to worry, folks. (*He reenters with megaphone in hand.*)

MANAGER. (*to the* GUARD) Our ladders aren't long enough. Call over to Centerville. If we can get the machinery working we may not need help, but won't do any harm. Stand back, folks. (*The* GUARD *goes off downstage right as the* MANAGER, *using the megaphone, calls up to the stranded riders.*) Just sit tight up there. We'll get you down. No need to worry about that. (*As the* MANAGER *moves along the ropes* LUCIUS *ducks under the barrier and heads toward the Ferris wheel. The* MANAGER *turns in time to see him.*) Come on back here.

LUCIUS. (*shouting as he exits*) Don't be afraid, Letty. I'll be there in a minute.

MANAGER. Get that darn fool.

ONE OF THE CROWD. Where does he think he's going?

CLARA JANE. (*who has been unable to see what was going on since the crowd pressed in*) What's happening, Mama? I can't see.

MOTHER. That crazy young man is climbing up the Ferris wheel. That's what's happening.

HOD. He sure is. Dag nab it. Good for him.

HENRIETTA. You would say so, Hod Tucker. Good for him if he breaks his neck. That's what you're saying.

LUCIUS. (*offstage*) Don't be afraid, Letty. I'm coming.

MANAGER. (*as he watches the offstage activity*) There, I think they have the motor fixed already. It's working again. (*into the megaphone*) It's all right, folks. You're moving. Be down in a few minutes. Lady, if you'll tell that idiot to hang on we'll swing him back to the ground before . . . (*There is a scream from offstage and then more screaming.*)

MOTHER. (*looking offstage*) Well, he fell. I could have told you he'd fall.

MANAGER. (*shouts to someone offstage left*) The first aid tent's down by the gate. Tell 'em we need a stretcher.

(*There is a general babble among the crowd.*)

ONE OF THE CROWD. (*looking offstage*) Everybody that was riding is off now. Nobody seemed to mind.

CLARA JANE. I'll bet the rose lady woulda liked to stay up there awhile.

MOTHER. Clara Jane, what nonsense.

HOD. I can't see Luke.

HENRIETTA. Of course you can't. He's flat on his back.

BARKER. (*who has been right up at the rope*) They didn't waste time getting the stretcher. There they are.

VOICES OFFSTAGE. Easy does it now . . . OK that's it . . . I got him . . . (*The* STRETCHER BEARERS *enter with* LUCIUS, *and* LETTY *runs in right after them.*)

LETTY. Wait now. You just put him down.

FIRST STRETCHER BEARER. I don't think he's hurt none, lady. They said he wasn't far from the ground when he fell. We'll patch up his bruises and he'll be good as new.

LETTY. (*drops down on her knees beside the stretcher*) Lucius, Lucius.

LUCIUS. (*comes to and sits up*) What happened?

LETTY. You fell, Lucius. You were climbing the Ferris wheel.

SECOND STRETCHER BEARER. Look, lady, we got to get this fella to first aid.

LUCIUS. (*remembering*) I was afraid for you, Letty. But I couldn't hang on. I got so dizzy. It was the merry-go-round and the barrel and the old windmill all over again.

FIRST STRETCHER BEARER. Look, mister, we can't stand here all day. You ain't the lightest load in the world, you know.

LETTY. Honestly, Lucius, it's small wonder you weren't killed. That was a foolish thing to do.

LUCIUS. No need to rub it in. I won't bother you no more. If you want Ferris wheels and merry-go-rounds and David City it's all yours.

SECOND STRETCHER BEARER. That's right lady, it's all yours. (*They put the stretcher on the bench and exit upstage right in disgust.*)

LETTY. (*comes to the bench*) Oh, Lucius, I got to tell you. This was a wonderful day, but the merry-go-round wasn't quite like I remembered. I guess you have to make your own magic when you grow up.

LUCIUS. (*swings his feet to the ground*) There you go talking about magic again.

LETTY. (*sits beside* LUCIUS) As for the Ferris wheel. I had a good long look from up high. The people on the ground didn't seem very important. The only thing that mattered was you climbing up to save me. And if the wheel hadn't started to move, Lucius, you'd have made it.

LUCIUS. (*stands up, a little shaky but at least he stands*)
I sure would have. I was afraid for you.

LETTY. I'm not sorry I came, but now (*She sighs.*) I guess
I'm ready to go home.

LUCIUS. (*takes command*) Come on then. (*He pulls* LETTY
up beside him.) I'll have one last look at the pigs and
we'll go.

> (*As they exit, the crowd, including* HOD *and* HENRI-
> ETTA, *begins to drift away now that the excite-
> ment's over.*)

MOTHER. (*who has gone over to pick up Clara Jane's
lunch pail*) I see your sandwich is gone, Clara Jane.
I'm glad you decided to do the right thing.

CLARA JANE. One thing sure, Mama, that egg sandwich
wasn't wasted. But like the rose lady said, deciding
can sometimes be pretty hard. (*quick curtain*)

PRODUCTION NOTES

The staging of *The Carousel and a Cold Fried Egg* can
be as complex as facilities allow. It would certainly be
effective if the rolling barrel, for example, could actually
be seen as the exit from the House of Thrills. On the
other hand, the play might be performed with less than
is called for in the script. The porch in Scene One might
be just a raised platform with potted plants instead of
the usual porch posts. For even greater simplicity, let
the action take place in the smooth dirt yard in front of

Letty's farmhouse with the house itself offstage. A rocker might well be out in the yard on a summer evening, and there could be an orange crate or something of the kind for Lucius to sit on.

Since the Ferris wheel, merry-go-round, and House of Thrills are offstage in Scene Two, the pace of the on-stage action is important. Fortunately things happen in rapid succession, sometimes simultaneously. However, subdued fairground sounds offstage—laughter, music, screams—will help keep up the tempo and convey to the audience the excitement and activity of a county fair.

The speech patterns are only suggested in the script. Except perhaps for Clara Jane's mother, most of the characters will drop the "g" on the "ing" words, and Hod might have a drawl. He is a slow-moving fellow anyhow. The barker is a fast talker, but his spiel can be changed as desired. The song Letty sings in Scene One can be chosen to suit the performer.

Mannerisms can also be given to the players. Clara Jane might be a nail-biter, especially when she is struggling with her conscience. She might also straddle the bench now and then.

Small props are indicated in the script. Clara Jane's lunch pail, and if a round syrup or honey can is not available something else might be used—even a brown bag. The lunch itself—the jar of milk, the banana, and the sandwich. The caramel corn in a box or sack. The mechanic's tool kit. The rope to hold back the crowd. The megaphone for the manager. The stretcher.

Research and imagination will open the door to costuming. Since Letty is identified by the rose on her hat, the flower is a necessity. Also because Henrietta refers to Hod's checkered shirt and cowboy hat he should have them. The barker's straw hat will be a "skimmer," while Lucius will wear the wide-brimmed one of a farmer. Beyond that there are no limitations.

NOTHING WILL RATTLE A REGNANT SOUL

SUMMARY

At the rehearsal of the junior high school graduation, Jill Avery "falls flat on her face" when she walks up to receive an athletic award. Her misery is magnified by the taunts of Duffy Morgan, who delights in the embarrassment of his classmates.

Counsel from parents and friends is of no help, and Jill decides to refuse the award rather than walk up to the stage again on graduation night.

In the end, Miss Pickering, gym coach and drama teacher, provides her own creative brand of support.

NOTHING WILL RATTLE A REGNANT SOUL

CHARACTERS

JILL AVERY, WHO IS GRADUATING FROM WILSON JUNIOR
HIGH

MRS. AVERY, HER MOTHER

MR. AVERY, HER FATHER

KATHY HOLMES, ONE OF JILL'S CLASSMATES AND A BEST
FRIEND

DUFFY MORGAN, ANOTHER CLASSMATE AND NO FRIEND
AT ALL

MISS PICKERING, "THE DUCHESS," WHO IS DRAMA TEACHER
AND GIRLS GYM COACH

MR. WINFIELD, THE PRINCIPAL

BETH CONNELLY, WHO RECEIVES AN AWARD

STUDENTS IN THE AUDITORIUM

OTHER TEACHERS OR TOWN DIGNITARIES AS DESIRED

THE TIME: *The late 1950s at the end of the school year*
SCENE ONE: *The living room of the Avery home. There is
an exit right to the kitchen, one at the left to the outside
and one at the back, off center to the right, which leads
to the bedrooms and the rest of the house. A sofa with a
telephone table on the upstage side of it and a coffee
table in front of it is at left stage. Opposite the sofa at
right center there is an armchair and lamp table. Other
funishings can be as desired, chairs, lamps, a bookcase
perhaps.*

As the curtain rises JILL *enters from the left. She is*

barefoot and carries a pair of high-heeled white pumps. Throwing the shoes to the floor in disgust, she plops down on the sofa.

MRS. AVERY. (*from offstage right*) Jill, is that you? (JILL *does not answer.*) Jill? (MRS. AVERY *enters, a mixing bowl and spoon in one hand. She sees that* JILL *is dejected.*) Jill, what's the matter? Is something wrong?

JILL. Not a thing. The graduation rehearsal was a huge success. I went up to get that stupid athletic award and fell flat on my face.

MRS. AVERY. Oh, honey. What happened?

JILL. I just couldn't walk in those dumb shoes that's all.

MRS. AVERY. Oh, Jill, I told you, honey. You've never worn anything but flats and tennis shoes. You see, the one-inch heels would have been safer.

JILL. Mom, you know I couldn't get those. Anyhow saying "I told you so" doesn't help now.

MRS. AVERY. Well, this *was* only the rehearsal, and I do have a suggestion, dear. Why don't you get out your good white flats. You can polish them up and wear *them* tomorrow. I'm sure some of the other girls will be in low heels.

JILL. There isn't going to be any tomorrow. I'm not going

to walk up to that stage again with old Duffy Morgan out there snickering his silly head off. I told The Duchess to just skip it.

MRS. AVERY. The Duchess? Oh, you mean Miss Pickering. She called a few minutes ago. Said she wanted to talk to you and would stop by on her way home.

JILL. There's nothing to talk about. (*kicks at one of the pumps*) Dumb old shoes.

(*The doorbell rings and* MRS. AVERY *speaks as she puts her bowl on the coffee table and crosses to the door left.*)

MRS. AVERY. That may be Miss Pickering now. (*She opens the door to admit* KATHY HOLMES.) Oh, it's Kathy. Come on in. (MRS. AVERY *moves back to pick up her bowl again and heads for the kitchen.*)

KATHY. Thanks, Mrs. Avery. (*comes well into the room and turns to* JILL) Say, where did you go so fast?

MRS. AVERY. (*as she exits*) Tell your folks we'll see them tomorrow night, Kathy.

KATHY. (*to* MRS. AVERY) I sure will. (*then to* JILL) OK, why didn't you wait up?

JILL. I just had to get out of there, Kath. I was so humiliated.

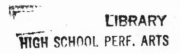

KATHY. (*sympathetically*) I know how you feel. Remember when I went to sleep in history and Miss Venderfort called on me. (*She mimics the teacher.*) "I wonder if someone can give me the terms of the armistice of World War I. Perhaps if Kathy Holmes has finished her beauty nap she would oblige. *Kathy!*" I almost fell off the seat.

JILL. (*laughs in spite of herself*) I'll never forget that. You were in another world. I thought I'd die when you said, "Let me have another fifteen minutes, Mom. I'm bushed."

KATHY. See, I've been humiliated too. (*She sits on the coffee table.*)

JILL. That was different. You didn't have the whole student body at your back. *And* Duffy Morgan.

KATHY. Old Duffy's a creep, all right, but don't let him bug you. Just be glad he doesn't have a crush on you like he has on Annie.

JILL. Yuck! That's for sure. I'd rather have him as a mortal enemy. Poor Annie.

KATHY. Speaking of Annie. Where was she today?

JILL. Maybe she's sick. I haven't had a chance to call her. (*She picks up the phone and dials.*)

KATHY. (*Gets up and moves restlessly about the room. She has nervous fingers and she picks things up and puts them down again.*) She said yesterday she didn't feel very good. You wouldn't think anyone would want to miss the rehearsal.

JILL. (*with the phone still in hand*) Except me. I wish I'd missed it. (*She hangs up.*) Line's busy. And you know, Kath, it takes a crisis like this to show you what kind of dumb things they tell you in school. We've had all these talks about getting comfort and understanding from your parents and teachers. Guess what mom said? "Why don't you wear your white flats?"

KATHY. (*halts her meandering and turns to* JILL, *aghast*) Oh, no!

JILL. She always was against those. (*She indicates the white pumps.*) When we went to buy my shoes she wanted me to get the one-inchers.

KATHY. Stubbies? Nobody got stubbies. This isn't grammar school.

JILL. You know who she talked to? Mrs. Roberts.

KATHY. But I.Q. Roberts is two years younger than anybody else. I'm surprised she didn't get Mary Janes.

JILL. She also talked to Mrs. McDugan.

KATHY. Doesn't your mom know Stringy McDugan's five-foot-eight? She wouldn't wear anything to make her taller.

JILL. Anyway, that was my comfort from mom. And dad . . . he's super as dads go, but not much good for advice. I don't think I've gone to him with a problem since the tooth fairy forgot my dime.

KATHY. I saw you talking to The Duchess. What did she say?

JILL. What do you think? "Rise above it." That's what she always says.

KATHY. (*dramatically mimicking* MISS PICKERING) "Let nothing disturb the calm poise of your regnant soul. Repeat it after me class."

JILL. (*going along with the act*) Yes, ma'am. Let nothing disturb . . .

KATHY. (*interrupting*) Remember the first time . . . when Annie said "pregnant soul," and we all broke up. (*laughs*)

JILL. (*enjoying the joke*) Guy, that was wild. Annie was mortified.

KATHY. (*sits on the armchair at stage right*) See, Annie's been embarrassed too. You aren't the only one.

JILL. Small potatoes compared to this. Anyhow The
Duchess wouldn't be any help. She's the one handing
out the trophies, and she thinks this sports award is
some big deal. Mom says she's coming over to see me.
To talk me into going through with it, I bet.

KATHY. I don't think The Duchess is all that hung up on
sports, Jill. When Miss Kennicott left she was the only
one who could take over the gym classes and finish
out the year. You know her only love is the theater.

JILL. All the worse. She's an actress. She can't understand
anybody being such a lummox.

KATHY. Well, you sure aren't a lummox on the volleyball
court. Gee, I wish I was getting some award.

JILL. I think you should have had one in drama, Kath.
You've got a lot of talent.

KATHY. (*Taking the opportunity to act, she gets up again
and speaks pompously.*) Thank you very much Miss
Avery. And to you, my dear, I shall dedicate my initial
Broadway performance. (*reverts to* KATHY *the school-
girl*) But you know I sure hope I can be as good as
The Duchess. I think it was terrible that her father
wouldn't let her go on the stage. What a loss to the
theatrical world. (*sighs*) I wish I could do Lady Mac-
beth like she does.

JILL. I'd be happy to have that gorgeous red hair of hers.

KATHY. Oh, Jill, that's a wig.

JILL. You don't know that for sure, Kath.

KATHY. I can tell a wig when I see one.

JILL. If it is, I wonder why she wears it. Maybe she
doesn't have any hair.

KATHY. There doesn't have to be a reason, Jill. People of
the theater are free spirits. They do and wear whatever
they choose. Just look at the way The Duchess dresses.

(*The phone rings and* JILL *grabs it.*)

JILL. Hey, Annie. Kath and I were trying to get you. Guy,
did I ever need you today. Where were you? You've
got what? Annie Patterson you're too old for chicken
pox.

KATHY. Chicken pox! (KATHY *stands by to catch what she
can of the phone conversation.*)

JILL. Oh, I know it's humiliating. And I'm an authority
on humiliation.

KATHY. Go on tell her you fell. It'll ease her misery to
know she isn't the only one. While she suffers alone,
you suffer before the masses. (*calls into the phone*)
Jill fell down in the aisle at rehearsal. She's inundated
with gloom.

JILL. (*into the phone*) You might as well know it, I guess. It'll be all over town by tomorrow.

MRS. AVERY. (*calling from the kitchen*) Jill, better get your clothes changed. I'll need your help before dinner, and your dad's coming up the walk.

JILL. (*into the phone*) Gotta go, Annie. I'll call you tomorrow. Bye. (*She hangs up.*)

KATHY. I'd better get home. (*heads for the kitchen left as she speaks*) I'll go out the back way. (*at the door she turns*) So, what are you going to do about tomorrow?

JILL. I think I'll go crawl in bed with Annie.

KATHY. Look, Jill, anybody who can smack a softball over the fence and lead the volleyball team to a perfect season ought to be able to . . . OK, so you're a little clumsy when you don't have a ball in your hand.

JILL. You aren't making me feel any better.

KATHY. (*takes a step or two back toward* JILL *and speaks seriously*) Well, I'll tell you. If you really don't want to go through with it, I could go up and accept the award for you. I could tell The Duchess you sprained your ankle when you fell.

JILL. Go on home. (*throws a cushion at her*) You're about as comforting as my mother.

KATHY. OK. OK. I'll go. (*As she exits right she speaks to* MRS. AVERY *who is offstage.*) Is it all right if I barge through here, Mrs. Avery?

(MR. AVERY *is heard on the porch offstage left.*)

MR. AVERY. Dad's home! (*He enters left.*) Hi, baby. How did the rehearsal go today. Anybody trip over his feet. (MRS. AVERY *enters to hear this remark as* JILL *runs from the room through the rear exit.*)

MRS. AVERY. Oh, Joe, that was the wrong thing.

MR. AVERY. What did I say now. I don't know whether I'm ready for a teen-age daughter. It was easier when she was three.

MRS. AVERY. Come on out to the kitchen and I'll give you a briefing. (*They exit and the stage is empty for a moment. Then* JILL *reenters. She is crying but seeing no one is in the room, she comes out to pick up her shoes. She puts them on, walks a bit, then takes them off and throws them down again. As she heads for the bedroom* MR. AVERY *enters and calls to her.*)

MR. AVERY. Don't go, baby. Wait a minute. Your old dad sure put his foot in his mouth that time. I'm sorry.

JILL. It's not your fault.

MR. AVERY. (*sits awkwardly in the armchair right*) Come on. Sit down. (JILL *comes back to center stage but she does not sit.* MR. AVERY *continues reflectively.*) You know, I fell down once.

JILL. You don't have to make things up just so I'll feel better.

MR. AVERY. Oh, it's the truth. I'd almost forgotten about it. Junior Prom. The dance floor was like glass, but I had to show off. Had a date with the prettiest girl in school.

JILL. What happened?

MR. AVERY. Well, I was trying out some fancy steps. I not only fell down, I took the girl along.

JILL. (*interested in spite of herself*) Didn't you just die?

MR. AVERY. I wanted to go through the floor. It was awful.

JILL. What did you do? (*She sits on the upstage arm of the sofa.*)

MR. AVERY. At first I just sat there. Then you know it was funny, but I remembered something my granddad used to say. "If you're in a sticky spot, boy, get on top of it. Always keep the upper hand."

JILL. Sounds like Miss Pickering.

MR. AVERY. Anyhow, suddenly it didn't seem too bad for the two of us to be sitting there together. When the band struck out loud and strong with "Keep Your Sunny Side Up," I started to laugh, got to my feet, pulled up the girl and we went right on dancing.

JILL. You were lucky though. No danger of the same thing happening the very next day.

MR. AVERY. Well, I had to face the girl. I was sure she wouldn't give me another date.

JILL. Did she?

MR. AVERY. She did better than that. She married me.

JILL. Mom? She didn't tell me this.

MR. AVERY. Maybe she figured it was my story. And you know, (*laughs*) she didn't tell me until years later that she went down with me on purpose that night. She liked me and felt sorry for me.

JILL. (*jumps to her feet*) Guy, Dad, you just blew the whole thing. Fat chance of anybody falling down to keep me company. And if I wear those heels suppose I do it again?

MR. AVERY. You'll have to laugh harder, I guess. Come on now. This will all be forgotten before your wedding day. (*He gets up, puts his arms around her shoulders,*

*and they head for the exit center back as the doorbell
rings.*)

JILL. I suppose that's Miss Pickering. I might as well get it
over with. (MR. AVERY *exits and* JILL *goes to the door
to admit* MISS PICKERING. *She is flamboyantly dressed
and not necessarily in the fashion of her day. She wears
what pleases her and leans toward spangles and beads
and brilliant colors. Her hair which is bright red is the
crowning touch. She sweeps dramatically into the room,
crossing in front of* JILL *to center stage, and when she
speaks it is with exaggerated drama and distinct enun-
ciation.*)

MISS PICKERING. (*turning to* JILL) Jill, my dear, you left in
such haste this afternoon. I simply had to speak further
with you.

JILL. Like I said, Miss Pickering, forget about the award.
I can manage to get up to the stage with the class to get
my diploma, but I'm not going to chance that walk
alone.

MISS PICKERING. That is out of the question. You must
come up and receive the trophy properly. It is a distinct
honor. And you will see, everything will go smoothly.

JILL. You don't really believe that. No one else does. Mom
says wear my flats. Kathy says pretend I sprained my
ankle. Dad says just go ahead and fall and laugh about
it. They all tell me what I should do, and I can't do any

of those things. Everybody has a solution, but nobody understands.

MISS PICKERING. Perhaps they do my dear. At least they care. That is why they have proffered advice. The difficulty is that advice may be sound only for the one who extends it. You have suffered a devastating humiliation. Of course it will be forgotten in time, but that is no comfort now. It is a mountain that has risen up before you, and whether you conquer it and how is up to you. The advice you can accept will be your own.

JILL. My advice to me is to get Annie's chicken pox.

MISS PICKERING. (*ignoring the interruption*) Remember the things we have learned in drama class. Hold your head up, chin in, and put one foot in front of the other, slowly, gracefully. (*She demonstrates.*)

JILL. That's easy for you, Miss Pickering. You're an actress. You've never tripped over your feet.

MISS PICKERING. That's true. I haven't done that. But, my dear, if you think I cannot feel for you, you are mistaken. Let me tell you something that few people know. You have heard, I am sure, the sad story of my thwarted dream, that my Victorian father wouldn't allow me to pursue a theatrical career. Nonsense. You know why I teach drama? Because it is the closest I can get to the theater. Yes, I tried. The community playhouses, stock companies, any place I could get a part. I couldn't make it. It was my voice. Oh, it serves for the classroom, but it simply would not carry to the balcony. The critics scoffed. "How can Miss Pickering be an actress of any note at all if she cannot be heard?"

JILL. Oh, Miss Pickering, I just can't believe that. Everyone says . . .

MISS PICKERING. "Everyone says." (*She sighs.*) As we grow older, Jill, we learn to draw the shades around us. We pretend that there were no failures in our past. We project the image we want others to have of us, and we welcome, sometimes we invent, the "stories." We are all actors.

JILL. Well, I can't invent any story about today. Everybody knows the truth, and they're all going to be out there waiting. Especially Duffy Morgan.

MISS PICKERING. Yes, there are always the Duffy Morgans of the world. Most of them with no talent of their own. But you will rise above them my dear. You will let nothing disturb the calm poise of your regnant soul. (*She crosses to the left exit and turns.*) Besides there are others who are on your side, the ones ready to give you courage. And you don't always know who they are.

JILL. I'm not sure, Miss Pickering. I just don't think I can do it.

MISS PICKERING. (*with conviction*) I shall see you on the
stage tomorrow night. (*She exits.*)

(JILL *thoughtfully picks up her shoes once again
and exits to her bedroom as the doorbell rings and*
MRS. AVERY *comes in from the right to admit* DUFFY
MORGAN.)

MRS. AVERY. Oh, Duffy, come on in.

DUFFY. Here's your paper Mrs. Avery. And if you don't
mind I'm collecting a little early this month. I want to
get my money turned in.

MRS. AVERY. That's all right, Duffy. I understand.

DUFFY. You'll have another paper boy next week too. I'm
giving it up. I've got a new job at the drugstore.

MRS. AVERY. That's fine. You're moving on. Graduating in
more ways than one.

DUFFY. I guess so, Mrs. Avery. Anyhow you've been a
good customer. Thanks. I never had to wait for my
money here.

MRS. AVERY. (*as she goes to right exit*) How much is it
again, Duffy? I always forget. Two dollars?

DUFFY. That's right ma'am.

MRS. AVERY. I'll be right back. (*She exits as* JILL *enters from the rear. She is still barefoot but has changed her skirt for jeans and is tucking in her blouse.*)

DUFFY. (*dropping the polite manner he had with* MRS. AVERY) Well, if it isn't twinkletoes.

JILL. What are you doing here?

DUFFY. Legitimate business. I'm collecting for the paper.

JILL. Of course you just had to collect today. You know Duffy Morgan, I'll get even with you. I don't feel very well, and maybe I'm getting the chicken pox. If I am you'll get them too. (*She blows her breath on him.*)

DUFFY. Oh, boy, how did you dream that up. You'd do anything to get out of tomorrow night wouldn't you?

JILL. I didn't dream anything up. Annie Patterson is spotted from head to toe, and I've definitely been exposed.

DUFFY. I've already had chicken pox, and don't blame me because you can't walk.

(MRS. AVERY *returns with the money.*)

MRS. AVERY. Here you are Duffy. And the extra is for you. You've given us good service. We'll miss you.

DUFFY. Thanks, Mrs. Avery. It's been a pleasure. I've always said the Averys are the nicest people on my route. And I'll bet you're proud of Jill here, getting an athletic award and all. I think it's great. (*He grins at* JILL.)

MRS. AVERY. See, Jill. You don't have to be afraid of Duffy. She's been worried about that rehearsal today. You tell her everybody's with her.

DUFFY. (*with exaggerated politeness*) Oh, I will. I will. I was just saying . . . (MRS. AVERY *exits while he is speaking and as soon as she is offstage* DUFFY *reverts to his usual behavior.*) . . . you're gonna fall again tomorrow, and it's gonna be real sweet. (*mimics the announcement of the award*) And now Twinkletoes Avery, the big athlete will stumble up to get her trophy.

JILL. You go on back under your rock, Duffy Morgan. (*She throws a cushion at him and he starts toward the left exit, laughing.*) I hate you . . . I hate you . . .

(*The curtain falls as* DUFFY *exits.*)

SCENE TWO: *The school auditorium the next night. The scene is presented as though the theater in which the play is being performed is actually the auditorium at Wilson Junior High. The house lights are on. Several members of the cast are planted in the theater audience—*JILL, KATHY, DUFFY MORGAN, BETH CONNELLY, *and as many "students" as desired. Before the curtain rises,* MR. *and* MRS. AVERY *go down the aisle from the rear of the theater to take seats close to the front but at the side. They speak to people* *as they go and perhaps* MRS. AVERY *could say to her husband, "Do you see* JILL?" *He might reply, "No, but I'm sure she's here." Other comments might be made which would be in keeping with this kind of situation. The house lights go off and the curtain rises to reveal a semicircle of chairs the back row of which is already occupied with teachers and town dignitaries. The front row seats have been saved for the honorees. There is a podium downstage right and to the right of it a table which holds a number of trophies and possibly the diplomas which are to be given out on this occasion.* MR. WINFIELD, *the principal, enters from the right.*

MR. WINFIELD. Good evening parents, friends, students. We have rather a long program ahead of us, and I will waste no time. The initial presentation to be made tonight is one we do not, cannot always offer. As a matter of fact, it was brought to my attention only this afternoon that we have a student who qualifies for it. Therefore, the surprise of the evening, the certificate of distinction for three years of perfect attendance at Wilson Junior High . . . (*He pauses for effect.*) goes to Duffy Morgan. Duffy will you come up please. (*There is some movement in the audience, some applause, and as* DUFFY *makes his way to the stage* MR. WINFIELD *continues.*) Now while Duffy is on his way, I will outline the program. First we have sports awards, girls and boys; after that the drama awards; then the recognition of academic achievement, the scholarships; and finally we will hand out the diplomas. We will try to get you home in good time. (*By this time* DUFFY *is on the stage.* MR. WINFIELD *takes a scroll from the table and hands it to him.*) There you are Duffy and congratulations.

DUFFY. Thank you, sir.

(*Again there is applause from the people on stage and the members of the cast who are in the audience. The real audience may follow suit as* DUFFY *is directed to a place in the front row of the semicircle, the last chair at the right.*)

MR. WINFIELD. As you may know, our talented drama teacher, Miss Pickering, graciously took over as gym coach when Miss Kennicott was unable to finish out the year. And it is Miss Pickering who will now present the girls athletic trophies. Miss Pickering.

(MISS PICKERING *enters from the left. Again she is resplendent in unconventional attire. Her clothes look as though they might have come from the costume room rather than a teacher's closet. A large plumed hat is the crowning touch, but it does not obscure the red hair. With her usual theatrical grace, at ease, self-assured, she acknowledges the audience with a gesture.* MR. WINFIELD *meets her at center stage, and as he retires to a chair at the middle of the semicircle, she crosses in front of him to the podium.*)

MISS PICKERING. (*turns to* MR. WINFIELD) Thank you, Mr. Winfield. (*then to the audience*) The girls athletic department has two trophies to be given tonight. The first, (*She picks up the statuette closest to her on the table.*) is for the girl who has made the most improvement in sports during her three years at Wilson, Beth Connelly. (*There is applause and* BETH *goes to the stage while* MISS PICKERING *continues.*) I confess it has been a bit of a challenge being a gym coach, and I trust my services in a field other than my own have been adequate. I am always happy to respond to the needs of Wilson Junior High. (BETH *is now on stage to receive the trophy.*)

MISS PICKERING. (*hands it to her*) Congratulations, Beth.

BETH. Thank you, Miss Pickering.

MISS PICKERING. The second trophy is, I think, one of the most coveted at Wilson. It is presented tonight to the best all-around athlete in girls sports. (*She pauses dramatically.*) Jill Avery. (JILL *doesn't get up and there is a stirring in the audience. Someone says, "Where is she?" Somebody else, "Go on." And still a third person says, "What's the matter with you?"*)

MISS PICKERING. (*calls again*) Jill Avery. (JILL *still doesn't make her presence known and* DUFFY MORGAN *who has been looking over the crowd has spotted her.*)

DUFFY. (*gets up and takes a step toward* MISS PICKERING) There she is, Miss Pickering, in the fifth row. There she is. (*He grins.*)

MISS PICKERING. (*brushes him aside*) Never mind, Duffy. (*She walks over to* MR. WINFIELD *and with a very dramatic movement bends down to speak to him. At that moment her hat and her wig, which had been securely fastened together, topple off into the principal's lap. The hair that is revealed is short and quite gray. The reaction from a real audience may be a moment of quiet which will be fine. The cast planted in the audience snicker and finally laugh as* MISS PICKERING *picks up the headgear and, holding it in one arm like a stack of books, comes back to the podium with great dignity.*)

MISS PICKERING. Well, Jill Avery, I intended to take my hat off to you, figuratively speaking. It appears that I have done more than that. Now will you come to receive the honor you deserve. (*There is stirring again in the audience and* JILL *raises her arm.*)

MISS PICKERING. There she is. Let her through down there. (JILL *walks up, slowly, head up, chin in. There is whispering all around. She comes to the steps of the stage and mounts them hesitantly, very slowly. When she gets to the top she smiles and walks with confidence to center stage where she is met by* MISS PICKERING *with the trophy in hand.*)

JILL. Thank you, Miss Pickering. (*out to the audience*) I'll bet half of you thought I wouldn't come up. And the other half thought I wouldn't make it. (*She gives* DUFFY *a smug look.*) But I couldn't let The Duchess down.

She's a really great person, not only calm and poised but just about the greatest actress in the world.

(*The audience claps and there is a very slow curtain to indicate that it is the end of the play—not the end of the graduation exercises.*)

PRODUCTION NOTES

The substance of *Nothing Will Rattle a Regnant Soul* is drawn directly from the modes and attitudes of the late 1950s. It was important to graduate from flats to high heels, and wigs were viewed with some suspicion.

The small props are mentioned in the script. Mrs. Avery, however, does not have to have a spoon and bowl. Anything to indicate her activity in the kitchen is acceptable. The objects Kathy picks up in her meandering around the room will be whatever is normally found on coffee tables and whatnot shelves—figurines, ash trays, books. Allow for several sofa cushions for Jill to toss at Kathy and Duffy. The trophies may not be necessary at all. Scrolls will do.

The clothes will reflect the fashion of the 1950s. Jeans were not worn as much then, but Jill would have them because she is the athlete, the tomboy. Maybe Kathy could wear glasses. They would be an asset when she mimics Miss Venderfort, who looks over them, and when she mimics Miss Pickering, who takes them off and waves them with a flourish. Miss Pickering's outfits are open to creative ideas as the script suggests.

A realistic set with walls and doors is called for in

Scene One, but the play would come off adequately without it. The furniture will give the feel of a living room,
and the ring of a doorbell is enough to tell the audience
that the left exit is the door to the outside.

It will be a challenge to integrate the audience of the
play with the actual audience in Scene Two. Other bits
of business with arriving parents and students may be
added as long as the interest in what is going to happen
is maintained.

You may not need the planted audience to initiate
laughter when Miss Pickering loses her hat and wig. The
real audience may laugh. They may also applaud at will.
The cast must adapt to the unexpected. Play it by ear.

THE BRACELET
ENGAGEMENT

SUMMARY

Ellen Carmody, a sophisticated movie studio assistant, comes home to her Hollywood apartment after a brief vacation to find that her twenty-two-year old houseguest, Kit, has become engaged. The complication is that the man is George Stanton, a fortyish playboy who gives out "engagement bracelets" with prolific abandon, and Ellen herself was one of George's early exploits.

The problem is how to open Kit's eyes about George and also throw her into the waiting arms of her college boyfriend, Tommy. The solution seems to be to set up a fake but melodramatic situation with the assistance of Janie Cobb, a young actress with her sights on the "silver screen."

A legitimate touch is added to the scenario by the entrance of Mona Page, and George's multiple attachments are jeopardized. The question is does the "trifler" end up with no engagement at all? Well, not exactly.

THE BRACELET ENGAGEMENT

CHARACTERS

ELLEN CARMODY, A SOPHISTICATED CAREER WOMAN IN
    HER THIRTIES AND AN ASSISTANT TO A DIRECTOR AT ONE
    OF THE MOVIE STUDIOS

KIT RYKER, FROM THE MIDWEST AND JUST OUT OF COLLEGE,
    SPENDING THE SUMMER WITH ELLEN, A LONG TIME FAM-
    ILY FRIEND

GEORGE STANTON, ON THE EDGE OF FORTY, A SILENT FILM
    ACTOR AND SELF-STYLED MAN ABOUT TOWN

TOMMY MARTIN, THE BOY FROM NORTH PLATTE, NE-
    BRASKA, IN LOVE WITH KIT

MONA PAGE, ONE OF THE LOVES OF GEORGE

JANIE COBB, HOPEFUL YOUNG ACTRESS FROM OMAHA

THE TIME: *July, 1928*

*The scene is laid in the living room of Ellen Carmody's
Hollywood apartment. There are two doors on the right,
one leading to bedrooms and one to the kitchen. Another
door on the left opens onto the outside hall. The furniture,
in keeping with the period is well chosen and arranged.
There is a desk with a wastebasket beside it at the right
between the exits, a love seat with a mirror above it
against the back wall, a coffee table with a candy dish on
it, occasional chairs and appropriate lamps.*

As the curtain opens, KIT, *in an evening gown, is kneel-
ing on the love seat before the mirror. She adjusts dangling
earrings and fusses with her hair which is short in the*

*fashion of the day. When the doorbell rings, she is star-
tled.*

KIT. Just a minute . . . just a minute . . . (*She exits to the
bedroom. The doorbell rings again, and again, and* KIT
*reenters. She still wears the earrings and she has put
on a robe which almost conceals the gown. She opens
the door at left to admit* ELLEN *who is weighted down
with two large suitcases.*)

KIT. Aunt Ellie!

ELLEN. Hope you don't mind answering the door. I hated
to fumble for my key.

KIT. I thought you weren't coming back till tomorrow.

ELLEN. Changed my mind. (*She puts down the suitcases.*)
The heat in Omaha was getting unbearable. I took an
earlier train. And I don't know why I always manage
to get a cab driver who dumps me on the sidewalk. He
might have known I'd have to struggle up the stairs
with these. (*indicates the luggage*)

KIT. Here, let me put them in the bedroom. (*She picks up
the suitcases.*) And you sit down. Have I got a surprise
for you.

ELLEN. I've got one for you, too. Don't bother about the
bags. Just get me a glass of water. I need an aspirin.
(*She take one out of her purse.*) I'm exhausted.

KIT. (*Puts the suitcases down again and starts off right during Ellen's speech to get the water. She turns at the door to the kitchen.*) I can't imagine why you wanted to go back there anyhow. Especially in July. (*exits*)

ELLEN. (*calling to* KIT) Well, it's home, and I had a vacation coming. Besides I was glad to get away from the studio. Everybody's panicking over talking pictures and I'm the one that's in the middle. Some stars demanding voice tests and others scared they'll have to have them. Directors scrambling to get stage people—which reminds me did a Janie Cobb call?

KIT. (*reenters with a glass of water*) Yes she did. Just a few minutes ago. Said something about your seeing her in Omaha at the Playhouse. She'll call again. She's at the Knickerbocker. Who's Janie Cobb?

ELLEN. Maybe just another starry-eyed kid who wants to get into the moving pictures.

KIT. (*grasping the meaning*) Ohh. You saw her *on the stage* at the Playhouse.

ELLEN. Right. Talked to her after the show. They were reviving *Pygmalion* and she was in a little over her head with the cockney accent, but she has a good voice. I said I was sure I could get her an introduction or two. My boss is one producer who believes the talkers are here to stay. Who knows maybe the gal will surprise us . . . (*changing the subject*) And speaking of surprises . . .

KIT. I haven't been. I haven't had a chance.

ELLEN. Well, let me tell you mine first. Guess who got on the train at North Platte? Tommy Martin.

KIT. Tommy! You mean he was on his way out here. Oh nuts.

ELLEN. I thought he was your beau. He's sure crazy about you. Made the trip just to see you.

KIT. Well, Tommy Martin can just go jump in the lake. (*She turns away in a gesture that reveals the gown underneath her robe.*)

ELLEN. Say, isn't that my new evening gown you've got on?

KIT. I wasn't going to wear it. I didn't think you'd mind my trying it on. I just wanted to see if it would make me look older. It does. And don't you think with these (*She indicates the earrings.*) I look like Joan Crawford? By the way, I've been trying to tell you my surprise ever since you walked in.

ELLEN. Fire away.

KIT. I'm engaged.

ELLEN. You're what?

KIT. I said I'm engaged.

ELLEN. I take it it isn't to Tommy Martin.

KIT. Of course not. Just because I wore his frat pin for a few months last year doesn't mean he still has strings on me. Besides, don't you think I know anybody else? This is somebody new. As a matter of fact, I met him the night you left. I've only known him for two weeks.

ELLEN. That's quick work for an engagement. And I'm not sure about Hollywood alliances. But OK, let's talk about the boy. Maybe I'd better have another aspirin.

KIT. First of all he's not a boy. He's an older man.

ELLEN. Stop right there. That means he's too old for you.

KIT. There you go, Aunt Ellie, jumping to conclusions.

ELLEN. Sorry Kit, but I promised your folks I'd take good care of you. Now I feel guilty having left you alone for two weeks. Of course you aren't a baby. If you're in love that's wonderful. They say an engagement ring is the dream of every girl (*She says this with a touch of cynicism.*)

KIT. Well, I don't have a ring, Aunt Ellie. I have a bracelet. (*She holds out her arm to display a gold charm bracelet.*)

ELLEN. (*startled*) You have what?

KIT. A bracelet. It's sort of a custom in George's family. Oh, he's just keen, Aunt Ellie. I know you'll be crazy about him.

ELLEN. (*quizzically*) George?

(*The doorbell rings.*)

KIT. Oh, golly, there he is. Will you let him in and keep him company while I put on a dress of my own? (*exits to the bedroom*)

ELLEN. As long as I don't have to captivate him with sparkling dialogue. What's the rest of his name?

KIT. (*from offstage*) Stanton, Aunt Ellie, George Stanton. (ELLEN *reacts to the name and then goes to open the door.*)

GEORGE. (*enters*) Kit here?

ELLEN. Red-Riding-Hood, you mean. Yes, she's here. (*She moves away from the door allowing* GEORGE *to come farther into the room.*)

KIT. (*from offstage*) George, that's my Aunt Ellie. Charm her now. She's very important.

GEORGE. (*taking a second look at* ELLEN) Say, you're . . . no you couldn't be? You just couldn't be.

ELLEN. Wanta bet? (*turns away*) The young and innocent will be out in a minute.

GEORGE. Ellen. Ellen Carmody. How long has it been?

ELLEN. Five years . . . and three months. If you'd like me to check my diary, I can give you the days and hours.

GEORGE. (*looking closely at her*) You haven't changed a bit.

ELLEN. Oh, I weathered the storm. I thought the sky was falling when my romance toppled, but Chicken Little only thought it was the sky.

GEORGE. So you're Aunt Ellie.

ELLEN. As if you didn't know.

GEORGE. I swear I didn't, Ellen. Kit talked about Aunt Ellie. She didn't mention your last name. It never oc-curred to me it could be (*hesitates in embarrassment*) someone I knew.

ELLEN. Oh, come now, that's hard to believe. Incidentally, I'm not really her aunt. Friend of the family. One, I might say, who is interested in the fact that Kit seems to be contemplating matrimony.

GEORGE. Actually the word wasn't mentioned.

ELLEN. I'm sure it wasn't.

GEORGE. You told her about . . . us?

ELLEN. As a matter of fact I haven't had time. I just got here, and this business was my homecoming surprise. When the doorbell rang the name George and a gold charm bracelet were my only clues. Not that I'd need to be a super sleuth to take it from there.

KIT. (*from offstage*) Hey, you two. You're awful quiet. I wanted you to get acquainted, but none of this silent communication.

GEORGE. She's a cute kid.

ELLEN. Your fiancée, George. But you're going to straighten that out tonight, aren't you?

GEORGE. (*smugly*) Could be up to Kit. She's not a baby. And you know I'm not even sure she'd believe any tales you'd tell her. She finds me irresistible.

ELLEN. Well, let me straighten you out on this, George

Stanton. You're not going to hurt her with one of your bracelet engagements. Remember, I'm a charter member of the broken hearts club. I'll find some way to open Kit's eyes.

(KIT *reenters dressed to go out, coat over her arm.*)

KIT. There now, didn't I tell you he was swell, Aunt Ellie. (*to* GEORGE) Shall we go?

GEORGE. I'm sorry, Kit. I just came over to tell you I can't keep our date tonight. I've got an unexpected meeting over at Warners.

KIT. That's not fair. You promised to take me to a swanky Hollywood party. You know everybody, and I'm dying to meet John Gilbert.

GEORGE. We'll do it another time. There's always a party. But come on, since you're all dolled up I think I can take time to go get a coke or something.

KIT. A coke! The least we could do is go to that little place down the street where they let you in the back door.

GEORGE. OK, I can use a drink, but just for a few minutes, I don't like to keep Jack Warner waiting.

ELLEN. (*sarcastically*) I'm sure he won't mind.

KIT. (*to* ELLEN) George knows the most important people

and the most exciting places. I didn't have a chance to tell you he's an actor and he's been in a lot of big pictures.

ELLEN. (*with mock admiration*) Of course . . . *The Great Train Robbery.*

KIT. I don't know that one.

ELLEN. A little before your time, honey. 1903 wasn't it, Mr. Stanton?

GEORGE. (*He is fidgety.*) Your Aunt Ellen has quite a sense of humor, Kit. She's handy with the jokes.

ELLEN. Who's joking?

KIT. I get it all right. I know what she's trying to do. (*to* GEORGE) She thinks you're too old for me, you know.

ELLEN. That's not all I think, but why don't you two go on out for your "coke." I have to unpack and my head's still splitting. Besides, I'm sure George wants to talk to you alone. (*She flashes a look at* GEORGE *as she ushers them to the door.*) I think he has something to tell you.

> (*After they leave she stands for a minute with a thoughtful look on her face. There is a sharp knock at the door and she opens it to admit an excited* TOMMY.)

TOMMY. Miss Carmody, I came right over. I couldn't wait to see her.

ELLEN. And you did.

TOMMY. I'll say I did. They walked right by me and Katherine didn't even see. She was so busy with . . . where's she going with that guy?

ELLEN. She and that guy are engaged.

TOMMY. That old man?

ELLEN. He's not that old, Tommy. Believe me. (*She moves to the desk and during the conversation rummages through the drawers obviously looking for something.*) I was engaged to him once myself.

TOMMY. You were! Well, no offense, Miss Carmody, but that makes him too old for Katherine. Didn't you tell her?

ELLEN. I haven't had a chance. This was as much of a surprise to me as it is to you. Besides I'm beginning to think Kit wouldn't believe me if I told her I carried a torch for George Stanton for five years. He's a charmer. That "old man" as you call him is a charmer.

TOMMY. Well, I hope to tell you he isn't going to take Katherine away from me.

ELLEN. (*who has found what she has been looking for—a bracelet like the one* KIT *has*) I thought I still had this. (*She reads the inscription.*) "To Ellen with my undying love . . . George." Hah!

TOMMY. What's that? (*speaking of the bracelet*)

ELLEN. All that's left of my lost love. (*She holds the bracelet up for* TOMMY *to see.*) Kit has one just like it. An engagement bracelet.

TOMMY. I'll punch him right in the nose. When are they coming back?

ELLEN. Soon, I think. He said he had an unexpected meeting. Wait a minute. I have an idea. I'll show not tell. Maybe if I get a hot little number to pretend . . . Janie Cobb! She just might want to rehearse a little.

TOMMY. I don't know what you mean.

ELLEN. You'll see. Make yourself at home, Tommy, while I telephone Janie and brief her on the scenario. (*She exits right.* TOMMY *paces around the apartment for a few minutes, helps himself to the candy from the dish on the coffee table, chews it vigorously and then mumbles to himself.*)

TOMMY. I'll punch him in the nose . . . right in the nose.

(*There is a pounding at the door.*)

ELLEN. (*from offstage*) Get that, will you, Tommy?

> (TOMMY *opens the door and* MONA PAGE *storms into the room.*)

MONA. All right, where is she? Where is the little snip?

TOMMY. Who do you want?

MONA. The Rah! Rah! Girl that lives in this apartment that's who.

TOMMY. You mean Miss Carmody?

MONA. *Miss* Carmody? Well aren't we proper. And who are you?

TOMMY. I don't think that's any of your business.

MONA. OK so it's none of my business, but there's something else that is. Where's your Miss Carmody?

TOMMY. I don't know why you're so mad, but Miss Carmody is a very nice lady. She'll be out in a few minutes. She's on the telephone. You better calm down.

MONA. I don't want to calm down. I want to stay all steamed up so I can speak my mind.

TOMMY. You don't seem to be having trouble doing that. Here, have a lemon drop.

MONA. (*brushes* TOMMY *aside and the candy spills and* TOMMY *starts picking it up as* ELLEN *enters from the bedroom*) Well, hello.

ELLEN. What's going on out here? (*turns to* MONA) Am I supposed to know you?

MONA. You live here?

ELLEN. I pay the rent.

MONA. You can't be the one. Is there anybody else. It's a little college queen I'm looking for—the one who's been running around with George Stanton. This has got to be the right place. Lover boy made the mistake of telling his landlady where he was going.

ELLEN. (*grasping the situation*) I'm beginning to understand.

MONA. What's to understand? I had a date with George Stanton tonight, but I'm fed up with that two-timing Hollywood sheik.

ELLEN. It's too good to be true. You're one of the loves of Casanova, and you've tracked him down.

MONA. Listen, I've been stood up every night for two weeks. Now I'm doing the standing. But I'll scratch that little dumb Dora's eyes out first.

ELLEN. Actually the dumb Dora is innocent. She isn't aware of Casanova's tricks—not yet.

TOMMY. I'm a little confused, but if you're referring to Katherine, she's my girl.

MONA. OK. You take care of her. I'll take care of lover boy. Just wait until I get my hands on him.

ELLEN. You won't have to wait long, but you'll have to stand in line. Tommy, here, and I have priority. Have a chair.

MONA. I'll stand thank you.

ELLEN. Whatever you say. (*She sits at the right of the stage.* TOMMY *sits on the edge of the love seat.* MONA *stands by the door, tapping her foot in impatience.* EL-LEN *speaks to* TOMMY.) I guess I needn't have called Janie after all, but an added attraction can't hurt the show. She said she'd be right over.

TOMMY. Things sure move fast in Hollywood.

MONA. All that baloney he gave me. I might have known he was lying.

ELLEN. It's a celluloid world. Full of George Stantons who like to double up on their romantic exploits. They think nothing of leaving a trail of battered and bleeding hearts behind them.

TOMMY. Well, Katherine's not going to be one of them.

MONA. I thought you said I wouldn't have long to wait.

(*There is the sound of steps in the hall.*)

ELLEN. And I was right. (*The door opens to admit* KIT *and* GEORGE.)

MONA. (*storming up to* GEORGE) Well, Mr. George Stanton, if you think you can give me the runaround you just have another think coming. "Can't make it tonight, Mona." "I'll be a little late tonight, Mona." "Have to meet my agent, Mona." (*She trounces him over the head with her purse with each of these last sentences.*) OK. Anybody can have you that wants to patch you up. (*She flounces out the still open door.*)

KIT. Who in the world was that?

GEORGE. (*with some chagrin*) There are a lot of strange people in Hollywood. Sounded as though she was out of her mind.

ELLEN. Sure.

TOMMY. (*with proper indignation*) I've heard all about you, Mr. Stanton, and I have something to say.

KIT. (*seeing him for the first time*) Tommy Martin! I

might have known you'd get right over here. You mind your own business.

TOMMY. You are my business, Katherine. I happen to love you. (*to* GEORGE) I'll thank you to leave my girl alone. I'm not a quick tempered man, but I said I'd punch you right in the nose, and that's just what I'm going to do, sir. (*He takes a quick hard poke at* GEORGE *and knocks him out.*)

KIT. What's the matter with you, Tommy? (*She bends to tend the flattened* GEORGE.) Oh, you poor darling.

TOMMY. He had it coming, Katherine. He acts like a big cheese, but he's a trifler. That woman (*motions towards the door*) knows it, and your Aunt Ellen knows it too, if you'll just listen to her. She knows because (ELLEN *gives* TOMMY *a sign to keep quiet about her association with* GEORGE.) Well, anyway he's a trifler.

KIT. I certainly won't listen to you, Tommy. I think you're all wet. Poor, poor dear. (*She cradles George's head in her lap as* JANIE COBB *sweeps in through the still open door and seeing* TOMMY, *the only man in evidence in the room, throws herself on him with great emotion.*)

JANIE. Dearest! (*She sobs.*) Why did you leave us. I came after you just as soon as I knew where you were. The detective agency has been searching for weeks . . . months. The children cry for you. Johnny and Hazel and Matthew and Baby Jeff. All of them. You've got to come back to us.

TOMMY. Now wait just a darn minute.

JANIE. Think before you say no, darling. I forgive everything. The nights alone, the unkind words . . . and look, my love, the bruises on my back hardly show any more. (*She starts to unzip her dress.*)

ELLEN. (*claps*) A superb performance, Janie, but you got the wrong man. It was supposed to be that one. (*She points to* GEORGE.)

JANIE. Gosh, I didn't expect to find him on the floor. What happened to him?

KIT. (*puts George's head on the floor and stands up to face* ELLEN) What's going on here? What kind of a show is this, Aunt Ellie?

ELLEN. Well, I admit Janie spread it on a little thick, but we were just trying to get through to you what a heel this guy is.

JANIE. I'm sorry if I loused things up.

ELLEN. It didn't really matter. We had some very effective takes before you got here.

JANIE. Too bad. I had some good lines.

TOMMY. (*recovered from his confusion*) You're a fine actress. You know that?

KIT. Actress! Aunt Ellie, you staged all this. I think that's terrible.

ELLEN. Not the first one, honey. She was the real thing. I never saw her before in my life.

KIT. You'll understand if I don't believe you.

JANIE. (*indicates* GEORGE) He isn't dead, is he?

KIT. (*gets down with* GEORGE *again*) The poor darling's still breathing—no thanks to him. (*She points to* TOMMY.)

JANIE. (*crossing to* TOMMY) You hit him? I might have known you were too cute to be the dragon. You're more St. George. Mind if I stay around awhile?

TOMMY. (*to* ELLEN) If you don't tell Katherine the whole truth, Miss Carmody, I will.

KIT. What do you mean, the whole truth?

ELLEN. (*takes the bracelet out of her pocket and gives it to* KIT) Here, honey. I didn't think you'd believe me. Especially about this.

KIT. (*who is still beside* GEORGE, *takes the bracelet*) Why, it's just like mine. Where did you get it . . . no, you're just staging another scene because you don't like George and you think I'm a child.

ELLEN. You might read the inscription.

JANIE. (*looking at* GEORGE *who is stirring*) He's coming to.

TOMMY. (*to* KIT) Why don't you ask him?

KIT. (*who has read the inscription and is beginning to see the light*) George? (*She shakes him.*) George, do you know my Aunt Ellie?

GEORGE. (*sits up in a daze and extends his hand*) Pleased to meet you.

KIT. George. (*She shakes him harder.*) Wake up. That's not what I mean.

(GEORGE *sits up, looks at* ELLEN. ELLEN *shrugs and says nothing.*)

GEORGE. I know her. (*He settles back down on the floor the way he was as* MONA *charges back into the apartment.*)

ELLEN. Hail, hail, the gang's all here.

MONA. Just something I forgot. (*She throws another*

charm bracelet at GEORGE.) No more Hollywood Romeos for me. (*She exits again.*)

JANIE. (*Picking up Mona's bracelet, she holds it to her wrist.*) Isn't it spiffy.

TOMMY. (*grabs it from* JANIE *and goes to* KIT, *dangling it in front of her*) Did you know he buys these by the bushel? (*He drops it in front of her.*)

KIT. (*starts to cry*) Oh, Tommy.

TOMMY. (*helps her to her feet*) Don't cry, Katherine.

KIT. I think I want to go home.

TOMMY. You can go right back with me.

JANIE. You know that was the shortest marriage. I never even knew my name. And why is it the good guy is always somebody else's fella. (*to* KIT *and* TOMMY) Good luck you two.

ELLEN. (*to* JANIE *as she walks to the door with her*) With your ad-lib talent and your tearjerker voice, Janie, you'll do all right in the talkers. Call me tomorrow.

(*They step out into the hall together.* GEORGE *has risen to his feet and walked to the back of the room. He moans, rubs his face, straightens his tie,*

*and slicks back his hair as he looks in the mirror
over the love seat.*)

KIT. (*to* TOMMY) If you want to, Tommy, you can hit him
again.

GEORGE. Hold it. I didn't know Aunt Ellie was Ellen, Kit.
Honest I didn't.

ELLEN. (*coming back into the room*) I guess we'll have
to believe him, Kit. Now that I've mulled it over,
George, I don't think you'd intentionally play around
with women who know each other. Too tricky.

KIT. (*to* GEORGE) All right then, just go away. And take
this too. (*She slips her bracelet off her wrist and throws
it on the floor.*)

ELLEN. (*to* TOMMY *and* KIT) Why don't you two go out.
See a movie. Ride out to the Santa Monica Pier. Just
get out of here. Everything's going to be all right, but
I don't think I can take young love just now. (ELLEN
pushes TOMMY *and* KIT *out the door. Then she turns,
scoops up the three bracelets from the floor.*) Well, at
least this puts three of these little trinkets out of cir-
culation. (*She crosses to the right and ceremoniously
drops the bracelets one by one into the wastebasket.*)

GEORGE. (*turns in time to see Ellen's action*) You know
I think I'm getting too old for this sort of thing. (*He
rubs his jaw.*)

ELLEN. (*shrugs*) You can't get an argument out of me on that. (*She picks up the suitcases which have never been taken to the bedroom and turns toward the exit right.*)

GEORGE. Ellen?

ELLEN. (*She turns to face him.*) Yes, George?

GEORGE. Ellen, I think you were the best of them all.

ELLEN. Come now, George. The cameras have stopped turning. And besides, remember I was in the original production. I know the plot. If you'll excuse me, I do have to unpack, and I haven't had a thing to eat. Be sure to close the door when you go out.

GEORGE. Do you suppose . . . I mean it's quite apparent that I'm free for the evening. Would you have supper with me? Just for old times?

ELLEN. (*hesitates and then apparently comes to a decision*) Now that's the most sensible thing that's been said tonight. I'm starved, and I certainly don't feel like cooking. It will only take me a minute to change.

GEORGE. No need to dress up, Ellen. We'll go down to Spaghetti Joe's like we used to. Remember?

ELLEN. Oh, I remember. But you forget. I've learned a thing or two since those days. I'll need to change all right, (*She smiles the smile of a woman who has every-thing under control.*) because you're going to make a reservation at The Brown Derby. (*quick curtain*)

PRODUCTION NOTES

The Bracelet Engagement is out and out farce. It should be performed with tongue in cheek and wild abandon. The characters are caricatures, the action verging on the slapstick, especially when Mona trounces Paul with her handbag and Tommy knocks him out with a solid punch. The success of the play will depend on this interpretation.

The fringe and feather flamboyancy of the 1920s reached a peak in Hollywood in 1928 with the onset of the "talkers" as the trade people called them. It was an unsettling year of change and speculation in the industry. All eyes and ears were on the "silver screen" where the heroines were marcelled and short-skirted and the men generally smooth-shaven and with patent leather hair. Joan Crawford, Clara Bow, John Barrymore, and Douglas Fairbanks were typical.

A little research will be all that is needed for appropriate costuming, manners, and speech.

There were dozens of words and phrases that were popular at the time, over and above the ones in the script. Kiddo, hokum, banana oil, hotsy totsy, everything's jake. More of this sort of thing might be put into the mouths of the proper characters, but it should be done with restraint.

Hand props include Ellen's suitcases, the water glass, the wastebasket, the candy dish which Tommy upsets, and the bracelets. The bracelets do not have to be exactly alike. If they all have charms dangling from them which glitter or jingle, the audience will take the word of the actors that they are identical.

If you find it necessary to present the play without a realistic set, it could be done. Exits and entrances could be without doors, and the production would be simplified.

FIVE TIMES SUE IS
JULIA BATES

SUMMARY

Almost sixty years have gone by since Frank Bates reputedly hid fifty thousand dollars in the old family home. The household now consists of the ninety-year-old widow, her son Fred and his recently acquired wife, Laura, plus Laura's eighteen-year-old daughter, Sue.

At the instigation of Sue, who has a rapport with the old lady, Julia's other children, Faye and Alex, return to look for "the treasure."

When the family gathers once again under one roof, there are hot words and cold shoulders. Is the money there? Is it found? The questions are answered in a finale which points up the fact that often the young and the old are drawn together, matched in understanding.

FIVE TIMES SUE IS JULIA BATES

CHARACTERS

JULIA BATES, JUST TURNED 90, SPARKLING AND SPRY WITH
    A SENSE OF HUMOR AND A ZEST FOR LIFE

FRED BATES, JULIA'S SON, 57, WHO MAINTAINS THE FAMILY
    HOME FOR HIS MOTHER, HIS WIFE, AND HIS STEP-
    DAUGHTER

LAURA, FRED'S WIFE OF THREE YEARS, WARMHEARTED BUT
    UNASSERTIVE

SUE, 18, LAURA'S DAUGHTER BY A FORMER MARRIAGE, JUST
    OUT OF HIGH SCHOOL AND PREPARING FOR COLLEGE

ALEX BATES, JULIA'S OLDER SON, 65, HEAVY SET AND HOT-
    TEMPERED

FAYE MALONE, JULIA'S DAUGHTER, 60, WITH A SHARP
    TONGUE AND A SELFISH NATURE

THE TIME: *One Saturday morning in midsummer of the
present year*
*The scene is laid in the living room of a large old-fashioned
home in a midwestern prairie town. Downstage right is
the front door and upstage right there is an exit to the
east wing of the house. There is an archway at the left
which provides an exit to the west wing, and in the center
of the back wall there are French doors which lead into
the garden. Julia's armchair is at right center and beside
it is a small table which holds among other things a low
bowl with cut flowers. There are other flower containers
about the room which is furnished for the most part in*

the mode of the era which produced the house, the mid-eighteen hundreds. There might be a small sofa down-stage left, several other chairs, another table or two, maybe a desk.

As the curtain opens, the doorbell is ringing insistently. LAURA *enters from the left with her arms full of towels which she has been distributing. She deposits the towels on a chair and goes to the front door to admit* FAYE.

LAURA. Yes?

FAYE. (*smartly dressed in a summer suit and carrying a small traveling case moves into the room*) You must be Fred's wife. (*She crosses in front of* LAURA *to center stage.*) I guess it's about time we met. I'm Faye Malone, Fred's sister.

LAURA. Faye! Of course. This seems to be a day for surprises.

FAYE. (*ignoring the remark*) What an exhausting drive. How anybody can stand this prairie country is beyond me.

LAURA. (*with good humor*) Maybe you've just been away from it too long. Is your husband with you?

FAYE. No, he had a big business deal on. Frankly I think it was an excuse. Believe me, I wouldn't have come in this heat either if it wasn't important. Where is mama?

LAURA. She may be in the basement with your brother

Alex, but I hope not. She shouldn't be climbing those stairs.

FAYE. So! Alex is here too. When did he come?

LAURA. Not more than an hour ago. He flew in.

FAYE. I might have known Alex wouldn't waste any time.

LAURA. It does promise to be quite a reunion. We had hoped you'd come last month you know for your mother's birthday, but this is just as good . . . whatever brought you.

FAYE. (*who has been moving about appraising the room, now turns sharply on* LAURA) You must know I had a message.

LAURA. No, I didn't. Your mother takes care of her own correspondence. She's a remarkable woman. Sometimes I think she has more stamina than the rest of us. I'll tell her you're here. (*She crosses behind* FAYE *and starts toward the left exit.*)

FAYE. No . . . not just yet . . . not if she's with Alex. As a matter of fact I'd like to freshen up a bit before I see mama.

LAURA. (*turns back*) As you wish. You can have the east bedroom. I'll show you. (*She crosses behind* FAYE *again and moves to the exit upstage right. Then she stops.*)

I forget. Of course you know this house better than I do.

FAYE. I should hope so. It's been the Bates stronghold for ages. And you've been here with Fred how long? Two . . . three years? Of course I was only nineteen when I left home. By the way I'd like my old room instead, if there's no objection. The little one in the west wing at the top of the stairs.

LAURA. (*a little taken aback*) That's Sue's room now, but . . .

FAYE. I keep forgetting that Fred picked up a ready-made family.

LAURA. If you'd really like to be there, it could be arranged.

FAYE. (*with irritation*) Don't bother. I wouldn't think of being an inconvenience.

LAURA. Actually you'll be more comfortable on the east side. It's cooler at night for one thing.

FAYE. (*like a martyr*) No matter. Wherever you put me. (*She crosses in front of* LAURA *and turns at the upstage right exit.*) I didn't say mama wrote to me. I said I had a message. Your daughter must have told you. (*She exits.*)

(LAURA *stands perplexed for a minute. Then she shrugs and picks up the towels from the chair. As she turns to follow* FAYE *off right,* SUE *enters from the garden with a basket of fresh flowers.*)

SUE. Where's Julia?

LAURA. I think she's in the storeroom with Alex. Sue did you . . .

SUE. (*interrupting*) In the basement? She's liable to break her neck on those stairs. (*She starts to work with the flowers on Julia's table, taking old blooms out, adding new ones.*)

LAURA. Sue, did you send some kind of message to Faye Malone, Fred's sister? She says . . .

SUE. (*with surprise and delight*) Has she come then?

LAURA. Just a few minutes ago.

SUE. That's wonderful! I was so hoping the two of them could be here at the same time, but it was really almost too much to expect.

LAURA. Incidentally, she wanted her old room . . . yours. But she settled for another. I told her you'd be willing to move. Faye doesn't exactly strike me as the gracious guest.

SUE. You mean Faye looks out for Faye? (*laughs*) I'm not
surprised from what Julia said. But she can have my
room if she wants it. If she can stand the clutter.

LAURA. No, she's all set now. But Sue, did you get in touch
with her?

SUE. (*hesitates*) Yes, I did. Last week. And Alex too. It
was sneaky, I guess, and I'll confess when the time
comes, but as long as it brought them here I don't care.

LAURA. Well, that's for you and your conscience, I guess.

SUE. Julia wanted to see them so badly.

LAURA. That's another thing, honey. Maybe you shouldn't
call her Julia. Just while they're here.

SUE. Can't see that it's any of their business, Mom. She
likes it. She isn't my grandmother, and I certainly can't
call her Mrs. Bates.

LAURA. I suppose you're right. I'd better get some towels
up to Faye's bathroom. (LAURA *exits right and is barely
out of sight when* JULIA *enters from the left and moves
into the room.*)

JULIA. Have you seen Alex?

SUE. No. Mom said he was in the basement, and she
thought you were with him. As a matter of fact I was

about to give you a lecture on taking those stairs. (SUE *crosses left to work with other flowers.*)

JULIA. Fiddlesticks. I can climb steps as well as Alex . . . maybe better.

SUE. Just the same the doctor told you not to.

JULIA. Well, you can save your scolding. I've been back in my room resting for the past hour. (*She crosses to the armchair and sits.*)

SUE. (*turns to her*) You don't know your daughter's here then?

JULIA. Faye too? I wonder what brought them . . . and at the same time.

SUE. You might as well know, Julia. I wrote to both of them. Didn't your son tell you he'd heard from me?

JULIA. Alex hasn't told me anything at all. I've hardly seen him. He poked his head in my room to say hello just after he got here. When he saw I was resting he said he'd talk to me later, and off he went. You wrote to them, Susie? What magic words did you use?

SUE. Remember the story you told me about the money your husband was supposed to have stashed away someplace in this house? Something like fifty thousand dollars?

JULIA. (*reflecting*) Yes, that it was. Fifty thousand.

SUE. I suppose I shouldn't have done it, but what I said was literally true. I said you were talking about the money again. And you were to me. I suggested they might want to aid in a new search . . . (SUE *falters, embarrassed at what she is confessing.*)

JULIA. (*crosses one leg over the other and her foot bounces rhythmically in a gesture which is typical of her*) Have I drawn the picture of my children so well? Of course that would bring them.

SUE. You said the most logical place for anything to be hidden in this old house would be in the basement, and that's what I told your son.

JULIA. So that's why he was in such a hurry. (*There is a great clatter from below.*) Poor Alex, he'll have the place torn apart. He was always the impatient one.

SUE. You're not mad at me?

JULIA. Of course not. It was a splendid idea. But did I tell you the whole story about the money? My husband, Frank, was a good deal older than I, Susie, and with notions about the man of the house handling all financial matters. He'd never heard of women's independence.

SUE. Born too soon is all.

JULIA. Well, of course Frank wouldn't have told me about hiding any money, and it didn't come up until he had his stroke. Then as it happened he couldn't talk. He scratched out a few words with his left hand, and he did seem to be trying to tell me that there was cash, a good deal of it, hidden away someplace. Not that it did any good. My brother came out from Chicago, and we looked a bit. Finally it was decided there wasn't any money at all.

SUE. Yes, you told me all that.

JULIA. You see I don't always remember what I've said any more. How I used to hate people who repeated themselves, and now I'm the one. The years aren't kind to the faculties, Susie. Don't ever grow old.

SUE. I won't mind if I can be like you.

JULIA. You know, actually I think we did look in the basement at the time. But Faye . . . what did you say to Faye?

SUE. I mentioned the old trunks in the attic.

JULIA. (*with almost childish glee*) Good! Good! (*There is the sound of someone coming up the stairs.*) It's been a long time since I've played a game with my children.

(ALEX *enters from the left in his shirt sleeves and out of breath.*)

ALEX. I'm glad you're up, Ma. I've been doing a little preliminary checking down in the fruit cellar. Looks like it hasn't been cleaned out down there in years.

JULIA. I don't suppose it has. Alex, did you meet Susie, Laura's girl?

SUE. Only by mail, I'm afraid.

JULIA. Fred's a lucky fellow to have found a family after all these years alone with me.

ALEX. (*nods impatiently to* SUE) Pleasure.

SUE. I'm glad you were able to come, Mr. Bates.

JULIA. Alex is my oldest, Susie. He's about fifty pounds too heavy I'd say but built just like his father. Besides his wife's a good cook. How is Helen, Alex?

ALEX. Helen's all right, Ma. But about this money thing. What brought it up again. What made you think of it now? I remember the talk and all the excitement when I was eight or nine, when pa was sick. Wasn't there some searching then?

JULIA. Oh, yes. We looked. We could have used the money. Freddy was a baby, and your father was so sick. Never did get well. Poor Frank, lay there three months with no communication. That was a long time ago.

ALEX. Didn't Uncle Ben decide there wasn't any money?

JULIA. Yes. "Frank's Fantasy." That's what your Uncle Ben called it, and I came to believe that too. We just put it out of our minds.

ALEX. The story was kept alive though, Ma. It was a game for Faye and Freddy and me for years. "Find the Treasure." Great kid stuff. Of course, I was the only one of us who really remembered where the idea came from.

JULIA. (*with a faraway look in her eyes*) That was a long time ago . . . long time ago. (*Suddenly she starts and indicates the flowers on the table.*) Aren't my flowers lovely, Alex? Susie never forgets to cut them for me. Have you noticed the garden. Just as it was when we were all here together. How your father loved the roses. The yellow ones died out though, and I neglected the others. Then when the dust years came, nothing seemed to thrive but the weeds. It all had to be replanted. But we did it, Freddy and I, and now it's just like it was.

ALEX. Ma, you are evading me. I came all the way from Muncie. What made you think about the money again? And why the storerooms? If it was the obvious place, hadn't you looked there before? Did you decide it might have been put behind the wall down there? Would pa have gone to that much trouble? (*As* ALEX

*talks, his voice gets louder and he keeps moving in
closer to his mother as though she can't hear.*)

JULIA. (*gets up and crosses to* SUE) You see, Susie, my
impatient Alex. Always the headstrong one, and what
a temper he had. I remember one day when Freddy
. . . no, it was Faye . . . had the measles, and Alex here
wanted to go to the park. How angry you were with
me, Alex. How you wanted to punish me for your disappointment. I had these Wedgwood candlesticks on
my serving board and . . .

ALEX. Ma, no one's interested in tales of my childhood.

JULIA. That's not so, Alex. Susie here is going off to college
in September to study child psychology. She is most
interested. Now, where was I? Oh yes, you snatched
up those precious candlesticks, one in each of your fat
little hands and stalked off to the bedroom. (*She acts
this out.*) Frankly I was frightened. I thought you were
going to break them, maybe over Faye's head. I couldn't
get to you in time, but just as I reached the bedroom
door you stormed out. "There," you said and your eyes
danced. "It'll take you a long time to find those things.
They're hid good." (*She goes back to her chair.*)

ALEX. So. This proves something?

JULIA. (*nods affirmatively*) Of course. For all your temper
you wouldn't destroy anything or hurt anyone.

SUE. (*laughs*) Your mother is full of stories about you and your brother and sister. I do enjoy them. It wasn't any fun being an only child.

JULIA. Did you know your sister is here too, Alex?

ALEX. I might have known Faye'd hightail it out from Lakeview as soon as she smelled money.

(LAURA *calls from offstage right.*)

LAURA. Sue, can I have your help for a minute?

SUE. (*calling back*) Be right there. (*She picks up the flower basket and exits upstage right.*)

JULIA. I've hardly had time to look at you, Alex. Come here. (ALEX *pulls up a straight chair beside* JULIA.) I wish Helen could have come and maybe some of your family.

ALEX. I wish they could too, Ma, but it's so damned expensive. We don't have the money Faye has . . . or Fred either, for that matter. (JULIA *takes Alex's hand.*)

JULIA. It's good to see you.

ALEX. I don't mean to be in a hurry, Ma, but I've only got the weekend. If I'm going to be any help on this thing . . . I still can't figure out why you decided to look again . . . after all this time.

JULIA. (*evasively*) Talking to Susie, I suppose. She is so interested in this old house. She is a fine girl, Alex. Freddy is very fond of her. Poor girl, she doesn't remember her own father. He died when she was two. Laura brought Susie up all by herself and she did a fine job . . . a fine job.

ALEX. (*disinterested*) Yeah, Ma. You know I hope this isn't some pipe dream. I remember Uncle Ben saying no man in his right mind would hide money in the first place. That's probably why he didn't believe the story.

JULIA. Oh, I could understand that all right . . . hiding money.

ALEX. Damned stupid thing to do in my book. Why wouldn't he just use the banks?

JULIA. No talk against your father, Alex. He was a good man. A lot of people didn't trust the banks in those days. Besides John DeWitt had the First National, and he and your father didn't get along. Anyhow he did what he did. That's enough.

> (FAYE *enters from the right. She has put on a smock to cover her clothes. She too is somewhat breathless.*)

FAYE. Well, here you are. (*She goes to her mother and gives her an impersonal kiss on the cheek.*) Fred's wife said you were in the basement. I went down the backstairs. (*turns to* ALEX) What were you doing down there, Alex. It looks like a cyclone hit the fruit cellar.

ALEX. Ma as much as said that's where the money is. I was trying to be helpful.

FAYE. (*in surprise*) In the fruit cellar? My letter mentioned the trunks in the attic.

JULIA. (*mutters*) Clever . . . very clever, Susie.

FAYE. What's that, Mama?

JULIA. Nothing. Nothing.

ALEX. Well, this is going to be a lively little weekend. How come Fred's not here. And how come he hasn't turned the place upside down before this.

JULIA. (*now playing the game to the hilt*) Oh, Freddy travels a great deal. He has so little time. And of course Susie and Laura wouldn't think of pawing through things that didn't belong to them.

ALEX. Still wouldn't think Fred would want to miss the show.

JULIA. He should be home today. He's due. Freddy works too hard, and he's done so much with the house in his spare time. Did you see the flooring in the hall? All new. And the fireplace in the library. Completely redone. Of course, a lot of the work Freddy couldn't do himself. The baths had to be torn out. Dry rot under the tubs. It's an old, old house but filled with memories. And I wanted to keep it as it was when you were little and you were all home.

(SUE *enters from the right.*)

SUE. (*to* FAYE) Mrs. Malone? (*extends her hand*) I'm Sue. Mother tells me you would have liked your old room. You could have had it if you wished. Can still. It's a nice room.

FAYE. It's too late now.

SUE. Do come see it, anyhow. I've got some hanging book shelves and an enormous bulletin board pops put up for me.

FAYE. Pops?

JULIA. That's Freddy.

SUE. My special name for him. But then he is special. Takes after Julia.

FAYE. Julia? Well!

JULIA. And why not Julia. It's my name. And there isn't anybody to use it any more. Last month, just last month, I was ninety. Ninety years old. There was quite

a celebration for an old lady. And no one to tell it to.
All gone. When I was seventy and seventy-five there
was still Hannah Martin and Mary Pennington and Ida
Spencer. And when I was eighty there was Hannah
still. But now I am ninety, and there is no one. Julia
is my name. (*During this speech she gets the faraway
look in her eyes and her foot bobs excitedly.*)

ALEX. Well, Faye, I hope you're satisfied. Now you've got
her off on a tangent.

FAYE. *I* have! You're the one who's been tearing up the
storerooms, stirring up the dust.

ALEX. Well, dammit, we'll never find out about the money.
I haven't got all summer. If I'm going to help, I can't
sit around on my tail while we talk about ma's name.

(SUE *goes over to* JULIA *who sits with her eyes
closed.*)

FAYE. Oh, you want to help all right. It's just like you,
Alex, to rush down here in a panic so afraid somebody's
going to find money, and you won't get your slice.

SUE. (*to* JULIA) I didn't know what I'd start, Julia.

ALEX. It didn't take you long to get here. And as a matter
of fact I could use money a damn sight more than you.
You and Jim off to New York one month, Miami the
next.

FAYE. Whose fault is that, I'd like to know? Jim Malone went through school right alongside of you, Alex Bates. Just because he had more on the ball . . .

ALEX. All right run me down. I'm just your brother. You never did have a thought around here for anyone but yourself. I didn't do so bad till Helen had that operation. Besides, what's all this got to do with it? I just wanted to help. Fred's never home. Ma said that. The point is why aren't we looking for the money? No, you have to make a big thing out of every word that's said.

FAYE. Oh, you are such a hothead, Alex. You make me sick.

ALEX. All right! All right! I'm a hothead, and you're Mrs. High and Mighty. A helluva lot of good it's going to do to get ma drifting back fifty, sixty years. First thing you know she'll be gone and . . .

SUE. (*who can stand the bickering no longer*) Don't! Please! (*There is complete silence for a few seconds.* FAYE *and* ALEX *are stunned at Sue's outburst.* ALEX *takes out his handkerchief and mops his forehead.* FRED BATES *enters from the right. All this action takes place simultaneously.*)

FRED. Hello!

SUE. (*looks toward* FRED *with surprise*) Pops! I didn't hear the door. I'm glad you're home.

FRED. Well, there's a warm welcome. But I don't think you'd have heard me if I'd ploughed in with a bulldozer. What have we here, a red hot Bates reunion? (*He moves to his mother's chair and touches her shoulder.*) Hi, Ma. Got your kids home, eh? It sounds like they're in top form. (*While* SUE *stays behind Julia's chair* FRED *crosses to* FAYE, *takes her hands, and looks at her with admiration.*) Faye, it's been too long since you've been here . . . five years, right? And brother Alex. How goes it in Muncie? Anybody bring any family?

FAYE. Jim couldn't make it, Fred.

ALEX. Helen hasn't been too well. You know how it is.

FRED. None of us can keep up with ma, I guess. Sue, your mother home?

SUE. Upstairs. I'll tell her you're here. (*Turns to go, but* LAURA *appears from the right and moves to center stage.*)

LAURA. No need. I saw the car from the bedroom window. (*She greets* FRED.) Good to have you home, dear.

FRED. No better than it is to be here. I'm ready to retire anytime. (FRED *turns back to his mother and notices her detachment.*) Ma, is anything the matter? Ma? (*No one says anything and he turns to* FAYE *and* ALEX.) Alex, Faye, what's the matter with ma?

ALEX. There's nothing wrong. There's just been a little excitement. (FRED *doesn't really listen to what* ALEX *and* FAYE *say. He and* LAURA *have gone to Julia's chair and hover over her.*)

FAYE. Fred might as well know what's up if he doesn't already . . . that we got these letters . . . that ma had the girl here write to us and . . .

SUE. (*interrupts as she comes to center stage to speak*) Julia didn't have me write those letters, Mrs. Malone. She didn't even know I did it until today.

FAYE. You mean all this was a hoax? (*with rising anger*) *You* just dreamed it up?

SUE. Oh, your mother told me the story all right, just like I said. And she did mention the storerooms and the attic as good hiding places, but that's all.

ALEX. I'll be damned.

FRED. (*to his mother*) You OK, Ma?

LAURA. I think it probably *is* just the excitement.

SUE. (*still talking to* ALEX *and* FAYE) I just wanted to get you here. Julia hoped you would come for her birthday, but you didn't. She was ninety years old. We shared the celebration because my birthday is the same as hers. To be eighteen is fine, but to be five times eighteen and like Julia . . . that's something. (*to* FRED) We sure did have a celebration, didn't we, Pops?

FRED. (*brought back to the conversation now that he is assured his mother is all right*) That we did. The town paper sent out photographers . . . The Chamber of Commerce made ma an honorary member . . .

SUE. And we had a buggy ride, a real buggy ride, courtesy of the county museum. There was a cake too, four tiers and ninety candles. We had trouble getting them all lit, though.

FAYE. (*as a kind of apology*) We might have come, but Jim had to go east on business. I sent a card.

FRED. She got it. The day after.

ALEX. Helen was sick, Fred. I never remember birthdays . . .

FRED. I understand how that is, Alex. I don't know what I did before I had Laura to remind me about things.

ALEX. (*back on the subject of the money*) So Uncle Ben was right all along. That makes me look the fool, pawing around downstairs.

FRED. That must have been where I came in. What are you talking about?

SUE. It was those dumb letters of mine. I'm sorry.

FAYE. It was childish, and I don't like childish games.

SUE. Would you have come if I just said Julia wanted you to?

JULIA. (*comes back to the present when her name is spoken*) Susie, Susie. It's all right. They're all here, and I thank you for the trouble. Don't mind that they quarrel. It's like old times. It's my family home again, just as they were. Maybe I'm to blame if they have faults. And frankly I enjoyed the game.

FRED. I wish somebody'd fill me in.

ALEX. Don't you know we've been tearing up the place looking for the money?

FAYE. And now we find out there isn't any.

FRED. Money? What money?

JULIA. Oh, the money's here all right, Faye. Your father's money is here. Ask Freddy. He knows.

FRED. Pa's treasure, you mean? Is that what you're talking about? (*laughs*) Oh, it's here all right.

ALEX. Damn it, Fred. I wish you'd stop talking in riddles. If it's here, where?

FRED. The flooring in the hall, the library fireplaces, the baths, the garden over the years, especially the garden. It's been used to good purpose.

JULIA. (*repeats, nodding*) Good purpose . . . good purpose.

FAYE. You did find money, then?

JULIA. Years ago, twenty-five at least. In your father's garden.

FRED. The garden had to be dug up after the dust storms, replanted. And there was the money in a strongbox deep in the ground beside the yellow roses.

FAYE. Why weren't we told?

FRED. It never occurred to us. Ma and I were here alone. As a matter of fact you and Jim were in Europe that year. Besides it really wasn't any of your business. Ma had great fun fixing up the house.

ALEX. And you let her do it? Pour all that cash into this old place?

JULIA. (*gets up from her chair*) Alex Bates! Stop talking as though I wasn't here. "Let me do it!" Of course he let me do it. It was my money. (*turns to* FAYE) And Faye, stop blaming Susie for her little game. I wish I'd thought of it myself. It brought you here and I'm glad of it. As for you Fred, you worry too much, you *and* Laura. Though I must say Laura is a welcome addition to this house. Now, I've had enough reminiscing. Come on, Susie, I haven't been out to the garden today.

SUE. Oh, Julia, the game was really your doing after all. You *hadn't* told me the whole story. If I'd known the money had been found, I never would have written those letters. (JULIA *takes Sue's arm and they go to the French doors at center back. At the threshold of the garden* JULIA *turns to the somewhat astounded group.*) Yes, I have my family all together again. And if you will promise not to bicker any more, we'll have a family celebration tonight. I'll take you all out to dinner. (*She pauses.*) I have a little money, you know, hidden away . . . (*She smiles broadly and* SUE *laughs as they exit and the curtain falls.*)

PRODUCTION NOTES

Five Times Sue is a contemporary play. Costume it as you wish. Substitutions can be made even in the one or two instances where specific clothing is called for—Faye's summer suit and the smock she puts on for protection.

Incidental props are noted in the script. Faye's traveling case. The flowers and basket. The flower containers. The towels. Although it is not mentioned, Fred would probably enter with a suitcase and perhaps a briefcase as well.

The dialogue should be the key to the portrayal of the Bates Clan, and Julia will surely upstage them all.

The realistic set designates doors to the garden and the front porch and archways to the two wings of the house. It would be better that way. Still the lines do indicate what is offstage to the right and left. The audience will know where a character is going when he exits into the wings. The back curtain, if it has a center opening, could be draped to frame the entrance to the garden, and there could be a painted view of the flowers and trees on the back wall. There is usually a way to adapt to your limitations.

WALK-UP ON CHRISTOPHER

SUMMARY

Three girls share an apartment in New York during the still lean days of 1936. Pat with dreams of the theater; Fran with dreams of the literary world; Jenny with no dreams at all.

A concentrated effort to impress Pat's great-aunt and uncle gets off to a bad start because of a talkative and over-zealous landlady. The situation becomes humorously disastrous when Fran arrives with the sherry bottle, token of her untimely dismissal from a thankless editorial job.

It is the revelation of Jenny's secret which confirms the value of the alliance on Christopher Street.

WALK-UP ON CHRISTOPHER

CHARACTERS

PATRICIA ALLEN, 18, FRESH FROM KANSAS AND A STUDENT
AT THE AMERICAN ACADEMY OF DRAMATIC ART

JENNY COLEMAN, 26, SHARING THE APARTMENT ON CHRIS-
TOPHER STREET

FRAN PETERS, 21, A YOUNG WRITER ALSO SHARING THE
APARTMENT

AUNT AGNES NORDSTROM, 65, A MAIDEN LADY WITH
WEIGHT AND DIGNITY

UNCLE PAUL NORDSTROM, 59, AGNES'S BROTHER

MRS. MC CASKILL, AGELESS, THE LANDLADY WHO HAS LIVED
IN GREENWICH VILLAGE ALL HER LIFE

THE TIME: *Mid-December, 1936*

The scene is laid in a walk-up in Greenwich Village. It is clean but meagerly furnished. A kitchen is partially visible through the doorway upstage left. A second door downstage left leads to the outside hall. There is a daybed against the left wall. Another door upstage right leads to the bedroom, and on the mantle above the fireplace, which dominates the right wall, there is a picture of a young man. A small dining table is in front of the window at center back, and on it is a cup containing a few loose coins. There are a couple of straight chairs and one arm-chair near the fireplace is flanked by an end table and lamp. On the end table is a copy of Gone With the Wind *and some Christmas wrappings. Since it is mid-December*

*the apartment displays a bit of Christmas decoration—
cards strung above the window, Christmas candles, holly.
When the curtain opens* PATRICIA *is at the window looking
down.* JENNY *is on the daybed easing off her shoes.*

JENNY. (*rubbing her feet as she speaks*) Do you see
them yet?

PAT. No. (*turns away from the window*) I sure hope
Fran gets home before they come. I can't imagine why
she's so late.

JENNY. I'm trying not to.

PAT. You don't think somebody got sacked again and
they're having another party?

JENNY. It's not beyond the realm of possibility.

PAT. Jenny, I'm scared. If Great-aunt Agnes doesn't approve of all this (*She gestures around the room.*) she
could ruin everything.

JENNY. She can't be that formidable.

PAT. You don't know. She's an old maid . . . everything
has to be proper.

JENNY. (*laughs*) I guess I'd better put my shoes back on
then.

PAT. You can laugh if you want to. Aunt Agnes may not live in Kansas anymore, but whatever she says still goes with my mother. And you can bet there will be a letter in the mail by morning.

JENNY. Don't worry about it, Pat. It'll be all right.

PAT. That's easy for you to say. You can do anything you want. Nobody reporting on you. Jenny, you know you're darn lucky not to have any family.

JENNY. Oh, Pat, don't say that.

PAT. I'm sorry, Jenny. You know I wasn't thinking of Max.

JENNY. That's all right. You'd better get back to your post at the window. We wouldn't want them to start up the stairs without a warning.

PAT. (*as she turns back to the window*) This place looked just great to me yesterday. Now I don't know. (*looks down to the street*) Oh, there comes a cab . . . yeah, it's stopping. They're here.

JENNY. (*who has her shoes back on now gets up*) I'll get the coffee on. You're sure your Uncle Paul wouldn't rather have a drink? I have a little Scotch. (*heads for the kitchen*)

PAT. (*still watching*) He probably would, but I don't know about Aunt Agnes. We'd better stick to coffee.

OK. They've paid the cab. They're coming in. (*sighs and turns away*) I suppose we should have had them to dinner.

JENNY. (*poking her head in from the kitchen*) With three cracked plates and no oven. As it is I asked Mrs. McCaskill if we could borrow a couple of cups.

> (PAT *bustles around the room, fluffing up a pillow, straightening a picture, stashing the Christmas wrappings under the daybed.*)

PAT. I hope we have enough cookies. We'd better not count on Fran bringing the almond cakes. Darn, darn, darn. Why did they have to come to New York right now? It took me months to talk the folks into letting me get this far from Concordia. Mom wasn't too keen on the idea. The American Academy of Dramatic Art sounds so Bohemian in Kansas. And Greenwich Village is even worse. I'll just die if Aunt Agnes spoils things.

JENNY. (*comes back into the room*) But her brother's a newspaper man. He can't be stodgy. And if she's been keeping house for him . . .

PAT. (*still nervously giving last minute touches to the room*) Oh, that's only been the last couple of years. Uncle Paul's been with one of the news services. Associated Press I think. Always off in some other part of the world. Besides, I'm not even sure Aunt Agnes approves of him. He's younger than she is. (PAT *goes to the hall door and looks down the stairs, then turns to* JENNY.) Golly, I can hear her puffing two floors down. (*exits into the hall and calls down the staircase*) Up here, Aunt Agnes, Uncle Paul. I'm sorry about the stairs. (*reenters*)

JENNY. (*indicates the rug in the center of the room*) Did you mean to leave the hole in the floor uncovered?

PAT. I didn't know what to do about it. If we cover it someone's liable to break a leg. If we don't it looks awful. (*She picks up the throw rug and looks intently at the floor.*)

JENNY. Cover it. I'll guide Aunt Agnes. You take Paul. They might not appreciate our view of the apartment below.

PAT. That's for sure. (*She throws the rug over the hole.*) That guy downstairs is a real doozy. There must have been a thousand beer bottles outside his door this morning. (*There are noises out in the hall as* AGNES *and* PAUL *reach the last steps and* PAT *goes to usher them in.*) Well, you made it. Come in. Come on in. (AGNES, *out of breath, stands for a moment just inside the room.*) Let me take your things. (PAUL *helps* AGNES *off with her coat but she chooses to keep on her hat and gloves.*)

PAUL. (*Shedding his own coat he stuffs his muffler into*

one of the pockets and then hands the wraps to PAT.)
There you are.

JENNY. (*who has been at right stage proffers the armchair
to* AGNES) I'm sure you'd like to sit down.

(AGNES *crosses to* JENNY *and sits down heavily.*)

PAT. That's Jenny, Aunt Agnes. Jenny Coleman.

(AGNES *turns to* JENNY *who is behind her and
wordlessly acknowledges the introduction.*)

PAT. And Jenny—Aunt Agnes and Uncle Paul Nordstrom.
(*exits to bedroom and returns*)

JENNY. I'm happy to meet you both. Welcome to the
Village.

PAUL. Our pleasure, Miss Coleman—Jenny, if I may call
you Jenny.

AGNES. Now I think I have my breath. I can't say I think
much of your walk-up.

PAUL. Don't criticize, Aggie. Just because you can't take
the stairs. The girls aren't carrying your weight, you
know.

AGNES. I don't think an elevator is too much to ask. Could

I have a glass of water, please. (JENNY *goes off to get it.*)

PAT. I know it's not the Lafayette. But it's comfortable . . . (*looks around*) Well, in a way.

PAUL. I think you're quite cozy here. And it looks like Christmas. How have you been, Bernhardt? Have they discovered you yet?

PAT. I'm only beginning, Uncle Paul. But guess what— Friday night we saw *Idiot's Delight.* (*very dramatic*) The Lunts are just superb.

JENNY. (*returning with the water for* AGNES) And last week we were able to get seats for Leslie Howard's *Hamlet.* Of course, we were in the last row up near the roof, but what can you expect for fifty cents.

PAT. I used binoculars to study Ophelia's face. She was so tragic . . . "I would give you some violets, but they withered all when my father died." (PAT *reads the line with emotion.*)

PAUL. At least you have fine actors to emulate.

AGNES. (*who has put down her water glass and picked up the copy of* Gone With the Wind *which is on the table beside her*) I see you're reading *Gone With the Wind* like everybody else this year.

PAT. I'm giving it to mom for Christmas. Didn't you just love it, Aunt Agnes?

AGNES. Interesting, I guess. But I can't see much point in dredging up the Civil War. We seem to be obsessed with war in this country.

PAT. But there's so much drama in it.

AGNES. Drama. Our memories can provide us all the war drama we need.

PAUL. You forget, Aggie. Pat wasn't born until 1918—after the Armistice.

AGNES. (*in realization*) Of course. And the proof of my age is that I have memories of even an earlier war.

> (AGNES *gets up and starts moving around.* JENNY *steers her clear of the throw rug and* AGNES *thinks she is assisting her.*)

AGNES. I'm all right now, Jenny. I can manage by myself. (*She waves* JENNY *off and speaks to* PAT.) Well, Patricia, let me look at you. Peaked I'd say and too thin. I suppose you starve yourself. (*to* JENNY) I'm sure she's told you her mother wasn't too enthusiastic about this whole venture. And I agreed with her.

PAUL. I'm not sure it's any of your business, Aggie.

AGNES. Of course it's my business. I may be only a great-aunt, but . . . (*There is a loud knock at the door and then without waiting for it to be answered* MRS. MC-CASKILL *enters.*)

MRS. MC CASKILL. I brought the cups.

JENNY. (*tries to take them*) I would have come down for them Mrs. McCaskill and saved you the stairs.

MRS. MC CASKILL. I've been climbing up and down those steps for longer than you been alive, young lady. (*She hangs onto the cups.*) I see your company's here. (*She moves into the center of the room and there are hasty introductions.*) Glad to know you folks. The little girl here said you were gonna look the place over. 'Fraid you wouldn't like her living in the Village, but I want to tell you Maggie McCaskill keeps a clean house.

JENNY. Of course you do. I'll take the cups Mrs. McCaskill. (*She makes another unsuccessful attempt to take the cups.*)

MRS. MC CASKILL. I won't have any crazy people in here. I've seen too many crazy people in the Village. That man down below you now. Gunderson he calls himself. Out he goes first of the month. All those parties and his strange friends. I hope they didn't bother you last night with their noise.

PAT. No . . . no all three of us went to the theater.

MRS. MC CASKILL. Where is the other one? The writer. (*looks around*) Not home yet?

AGNES. That's right. You did say there were three of you.

PAT. Fran. She's a little late tonight. She works for a big publishing house and . . .

MRS. MC CASKILL. Ha! That outfit. (*She crosses to* PAUL.) You wouldn't believe it mister. Hires these girls to read the stuff that comes over the transom . . . three weeks trial basis see, no pay.

PAT. Uncle Paul isn't interested in . . .

MRS. MC CASKILL. Sure he is. (*goes right on*) They say they want to know if the girls'll work out. Never do, of course. Free help. That's what they want. And then the poor kids are out pounding the pavement again. Almost a month wasted and all they get for their time is a farewell shindig.

PAUL. We know there's a great deal of inequity in the country, Mrs. McCaskill.

JENNY. In the world.

PAT. (*still trying to build up* FRAN) Fran's a writer too. She has a story out now at *The Atlantic*.

MRS. MC CASKILL. Writers. Talk about writers. My husband, rest his soul, was a poet, and we saw writers come and go. The best of them and the worst of them. Amy Lowell, E. A. Robinson, Sinclair Lewis, Edna Millay, Joe Shackey . . .

JENNY. (*laughs*) Shackey? Who's Joe Shackey?

MRS. MC CASKILL. One of the worst. Poor old Shackey. If I hadn't let him put his feet under my table three nights a week he would have starved.

PAUL. I guess some of the best starved now and then.

MRS. MC CASKILL. And that's the truth, sir. Everyone didn't get the reception of Eugene O'Neill. The Village was good to him from the start.

JENNY. That's all for tonight, Mrs. McCaskill. We'll have to save Eugene O'Neill for another time. (*She literally wrenches the cups from Mrs. McCaskill's hands.*) I wonder—if you see Frances on your way down tell her to hurry.

PAT. I'll bring your cups back in the morning. (*There are good-byes and* PAUL, *the perfect gentleman, goes out the door with* MRS. MC CASKILL *who keeps on chattering.*)

MRS. MC CASKILL. The Village just isn't what it used to be fifteen—twenty years ago. Oh, I remember Willa Cather, Dreiser, O. Henry. To say nothing of the actors . . .

(*They are finally out of earshot and there is a moment of quiet in the apartment.*)

JENNY. Well, now we can have some coffee. I know you folks have had dinner. Probably a late one, but Pat tells me you are like all good Danes when it comes to coffee.

AGNES. (*who has been roaming around the apartment most of the time, looking off to other rooms*) Thank you. It is rather close in here, and I have a headache. Coffee would be good. (JENNY *exits to the kitchen and* AGNES *turns to* PAT.) Patricia, how did you girls get together—and here. (*looks around with a frown*)

PAT. Fran went to school with Sue Picking. You remember Sue, my friend?

AGNES. Picking. Sue Picking. Yes, I think I do.

PAT. Well, Sue's still holding out at college. Fran only did two years. A Missouri girl's school is no place for a writer. She was in a girl's club here in New York, and Sue told me to look her up. We found this apartment together. An apartment is so much more fun. And cheaper too when you do your cooking.

PAUL. (*reenters chuckling*) I like your Mrs. McCaskill. Dyed-in-the-wool Villager. Knows the place back to Washington Irving.

JENNY. (*coming in with a tray*) I'm surprised you escaped from her. She's a good old soul though.

AGNES. (*ignoring the interruption*) The writer girl. How old is she?

PAT. That's what's special. She's got so much talent, and she's only twenty-one.

AGNES. Another child. And you, Jenny. I suppose you paint or dance or some such thing. You're planning a career too, I suppose?

JENNY. Well, I certainly hope it's not at Macy's. My feet would rebel.

AGNES. I will say you look older than Patricia. I'd hoped one of you would have a little maturity.

PAUL. Now Agnes, that's impertinent. Age is unmentionable among women. You should know that.

AGNES. Women! Posh. When you're as young as they are you're all eagerness for the years to pass. Can't wait to be older.

JENNY. I'm afraid I'm not that young, Miss Nordstrom.

AGNES. And are you from Kansas too?

JENNY. No. I'm not sure I can really claim any roots. I've

been in New York for almost two years. Living in a
small hotel. But that wasn't any place for me. I needed
a kitchen. I think I was cut out for pots and pans.
Poking around looking for an apartment I came upon
this place. The girls needed a third person to meet the
rent, and Mrs. McCaskill suggested I might be the
answer. I guess my recommendations were adequate.

PAT. I don't know what we'd do without Jenny. She's so
efficient. And we're always crying on her shoulder.

AGNES. And your family approves of this. (*She indicates
the room.*)

JENNY. No family, Miss Nordstrom, unless you want to
count the faculty of Mrs. Webb's Boarding School and
the alumni of Radcliffe. You see I was lucky enough to
have been left a solid trust fund to get me through
school.

PAT. Jenny may be working at Macy's, Aunt Agnes, but
she's really a teacher.

JENNY. (*laughs*) Without any experience of course. In
1932 no one wanted an English teacher right out of
college. There were plenty of old-timers lined up for
the vacancies.

PAT. She's been to Europe too. Spent two years in Germany.

PAUL. (*with interest*) Germany?

JENNY. With no prospects here, I got a job through the school as tutor-governess with a family in Berlin. But that's water under the bridge. I came back early in 1935. Since then Macy's. It's a job. I have no plans beyond that right now.

AGNES. (*who has been moving about the apartment all this time, pauses at the mantle and picks up the picture*) And your young man? Forgive my being nosy, but I see by the affectionate signature that it is your young man. What does he think? What are his plans?

JENNY. (*with a note of irritation in her voice*) He's not here—I left him in Berlin.

AGNES. Well, that's not so final. (*returns the picture to its place*) At least you young people don't have war to contend with.

JENNY. (*obviously upset*) Please . . . (*She exits to the kitchen.*)

PAUL. (*gets up and crosses to* AGNES) Agnes, you have the finesse of an amoeba. Come on sit down and finish your coffee. (AGNES *resumes her place in the armchair.*)

PAT. She doesn't talk about Max, Aunt Agnes. He's dead. He was a medical student and there was some kind of

trouble—protest. He was Jewish. I don't know much
about it, but he was killed.

> (*While* PAT *is talking* PAUL *moves to the mantle
> and looks seriously at the picture, rubbing his chin
> in a thoughtful gesture.*)
> (JENNY *returns with more coffee and there is an
> embarrassed silence finally broken by* AGNES.)

AGNES. I'm sorry, Jenny. Forgive a tactless old woman.

JENNY. It's all right. I shouldn't be vulnerable. (*She fills
Agnes's cup.*) May I fill your cup, Mr. Nordstrom?

PAUL. Yes, thanks. (*He accepts more coffee and is about
to speak but changes his mind.*)

PAT. (*in an effort to change the subject*) I had a letter
from mother today. She says dad's practice is thriving.
Everyone seems to be having babies or tonsillectomies.
Only thing is nobody pays him in money. He has three
pigs and a donkey he doesn't know what to do with,
and he's had the house painted twice. (*laughs*)

AGNES. I don't know what's happening in this country.
And that man in Washington isn't helping much.

PAUL. Well, your fellow from Kansas tried to get a shot
at it, but couldn't pull it off. I'm not sure there are
any easy answers.

JENNY. I don't think Roosevelt's the man we have to worry about.

PAUL. I agree with you Jenny. I had a special assignment in Germany in '34. I didn't like the way things looked even then. And Hitler's march into the Rhineland this year was foreboding. Things seem to be getting worse. (*There are sounds on the stairs followed by a loud shout.*)

FRAN. (*banging on the door*) Knock! Knock!

PAT. (*opening the door*) Fran!

FRAN. You didn't play the game. (*She enters, a little tipsy and with both arms full—a bottle of sherry in one hand and papers and books in the other.*) You were supposed to say . . . "Who's there?" And then I say "Donna." And then . . .

JENNY. (*patiently*) OK, Fran. Donna who?

FRAN. (*sweeping into the room*) Donna have a job anymore.

PAT. Oh no, Fran, not you.

FRAN. Yep. No mistake.

PAT. And I suppose you forgot the cakes from Louie's.

FRAN. No cakes, my pet. But little old Fran brought the bottle. They always give the bottle to the retiring member of the staff. Best sherry in the country. And it was a perfectly wonderful party. I wish you could have been there. (FRAN *moves a little uncertainly across the room and stumbles against Paul's feet.*) Excuse me, sir. The room's too crowded. It's always crowded. Pat, you little old dog, you'll have to stop bringing your boyfriends in.

(JENNY *exits to the kitchen to get a cup for* FRAN.)

PAT. (*miserably*) Frances! That's my Uncle Paul, and this is my Aunt Agnes. Did you forget they were coming tonight?

FRAN. (*claps her hand over her mouth*) Ohhh! I sure enough did. I'm so sorry, Aunt Agnes . . . Uncle Paul. (*She weaves a little.*)

PAUL. Don't you want to sit down, young lady?

FRAN. Don't you worry about me. I'm a little light-headed, but it's not altogether the sherry. Don't you believe it. I'm naturally a little balmy.

AGNES. This is the girl who writes for *The Atlantic?*

FRAN. Who's been spreading that propaganda? I'm the original confessioner—hard luck Hannah of the pulps. Hannah Halliger, that's me. I've got the letters from the editors to prove it. So you're Aunt Agnes. I'm delighted to know you. (*She looks her over.*) Now you don't look like a dragon. (*She curls up on the daybed, feet crossed beneath her.*)

JENNY. (*returning from the kitchen with a cup of coffee for* FRAN) Here you are Frances. We didn't really need the cakes. There are plenty of cookies *and* coffee.

FRAN. (*takes the cup and sets it on the floor*) *The Atlantic,* she says. If *The Atlantic* ever takes a story of mine, I'll really get tight. (*She leans over and pulls a battered suitcase from under the daybed.*) Got to dig Hannah out of the files. Good old Hannah. (*She opens the case and brings out a sheaf of papers.*)

JENNY. Not now, Fran.

FRAN. (*ignoring her*) I don't suppose anybody's told you about Hannah. She's not a bad girl, but the messes she gets herself into to provide my bread and butter. Just listen to this. "They didn't understand me. My mother sat there with a stern cold face, and my father said, 'You needn't come back through that door if you leave this house tonight. You are no longer a daughter of mine.' If only someone would understand me." (FRAN *puts a good deal of expression into the lines.*)

PAUL. Have you ever considered joining Pat over at the Academy?

PAT. (*apologetically*) Well, someone gets paid to write those things. It might as well be Fran. Besides, you wait. Someday *The Atlantic* will buy.

(PAUL *chuckles and* FRAN *continues as though no one has interrupted.*)

FRAN. "If someone had only told me how impossible it is to erase a single day of one's life. No one understood me. No one could see why I thought my future depended on slipping out into the night to meet Montgomery. And now here was I without honor and without love."

PAT. Jenny, can't you stop her?

JENNY. I tried. (*shrugs*)

FRAN. Poor little old Hannah. She's been expelled from school, lost two husbands, had three babies, and fallen into the hands of the white slaver. Now she'll have to suffer again. (FRAN, *in her enthusiasm, has gotten up and moved about the room. With these last words she trips in the hole under the rug and sits down with a thud.*) Now who the devil covered the hole of Calcutta?

PAT. Oh, Fran, I'm sorry.

(PAUL *moves to help* FRAN *to her feet.*)

FRAN. Don't bother, sir. I'll just stay here. Hand me my coffee. (PAUL *picks her cup up off the floor and hands it to her while* PAT *pushes the suitcase back under the bed.*)

JENNY. I think Hannah's suffered enough for tonight. (*laughs*) Mr. Nordstrom, Pat tells me you're with one of the news services.

PAUL. I was until '34. It got a little too strenuous for me. As a matter of fact I bought an interest in this little paper upstate. Still write a political column and an editorial now and then. Keep my hand in.

AGNES. He has too much to say not to keep a hand in.

JENNY. Sounds like a good life. Do you come to New York often?

PAUL. Not if I can help it. A bit of business now and then. I have an appointment in the morning and then we'll be on our way home.

AGNES. New York is too uncertain in December. And if there's snow it's slush as soon as it falls. If I'm going to have snow, I want it to stay awhile.

PAT. (*to* FRAN) Want more coffee? (*then to the others*) Anybody?

AGNES. I really think we'd better run along. My headache's no better, and you girls must be tired. (*looks pointedly at* FRAN)

JENNY. Don't rush away. You've seen us at our worst now.

AGNES. I'll call you in the morning before we leave.

PAT. I'll get your things. (*exits to the bedroom*)

FRAN. (*getting up*) Well, enough brooding. I've wasted three weeks. Can't waste the night away.

(PAT *comes back in with Agnes's coat and Paul's overcoat.*)

JENNY. Come again now.

FRAN. Next time we'll have the party here.

PAUL. We'll keep in touch. (*to* FRAN) Good-bye, young lady. There'll be a better job around the corner. (*to* JENNY) Yes, we'll keep in touch.

PAT. When I write to the folks I'll tell them you were here.

AGNES. I shall write your mother too. (*general good-byes,* PAUL *and* AGNES *exit*)

PAT. Well, I guess that's that. I'll probably be back in Concordia before Christmas.

FRAN. Your uncle's a peach.

JENNY. I think Aunt Agnes is all right too. Solid. Someone to lean on. I suppose we did come off on the irresponsible side.

FRAN. I really loused it up, didn't I?

PAT. You didn't exactly help.

JENNY. (*picking up the coffee cups*) Why don't you two go down after a paper. And we're out of aspirin. Aunt Agnes isn't the only one with a head.

FRAN. If you mean me, the glow's all gone. I'm sadly sober. Lordy, I'm sorry, Pat. It was losing the job that did it. Job, she says. But I had hoped that I might be the one who'd "work out." And they did keep me in carbon paper. Besides how did I know you'd covered the hole.

PAT. Forget it, Fran. If I just didn't have to go back to Kansas.

JENNY. You're lucky, Pat, to have a Kansas to go to.

FRAN. Maybe we'd better go for the paper, Pat, before I start to bawl. (FRAN *and* PAT *exit*)

> (*An organ grinder is heard in the street and* JENNY *goes to the window. She takes a coin from the cup on the table and tosses it out.*)

JENNY. Here, Tony, catch. (*She stands at the window listening to the music. There is a knock at the door.*) It's open. Come in. (PAUL *enters, leaving the door ajar behind him.*)

PAUL. I put Agnes in a cab on the pretense of wanting to walk to the hotel. I had something I wanted to say.

JENNY. The girls have gone for a paper, Mr. Nordstrom. You must have passed them.

PAUL. I did. But I told them to go on—that I had just forgotten my muffler. Actually I was glad it worked that way.

JENNY. We made a fiasco of it, didn't we?

PAUL. I told Pat everything would be all right. Agnes may rant a bit, but I think I can take care of her. I really wanted to see you alone.

JENNY. Oh?

(PAUL *walks to the fireplace and studies Max's picture.*)

PAUL. I thought your Max looked familiar. And you too for that matter. I almost said something earlier, but Agnes blundered on about plans and wars and I thought I should keep quiet.

JENNY. You knew Max?

PAUL. My last stint with AP took me to Berlin. I was doing a story on what was happening there. Yes, I met your young man. I didn't know he'd been killed. I'm sorry, very sorry. He told me about you. Showed me your picture. I suppose that's why I remembered him. It was only our first meeting. Anyhow I am pleased now to meet his girl.

JENNY. Not his girl, Mr. Nordstrom. His wife.

PAUL. Yes. I knew that too. I wasn't sure why he told me.

JENNY. He must have liked you. And you were an American. I suppose he wanted to tell someone, and there weren't many people he could trust. By mid '34 we weren't able to spend much time together, but I do remember his saying he'd met an American newsman. He told me if anything happened to him I was to leave Germany at once. Under my own passport. The girls don't even know about this, and I'd just as soon keep it that way.

PAUL. They'd understand. Might even help. I think there's strength for all of you in your threesome here in the Village.

JENNY. I hadn't thought of it that way.

PAUL. Don't just give, Jenny. Take a little too. But if the time comes that you want to leave New York, let me know. Our town might be worth a try.

JENNY. I may take you up on that. Thank you, Mr. Nordstrom. In fact do you think we should borrow a bit of
Fran's sherry to drink to it?

PAUL. If you hadn't suggested it I would have.

JENNY. Fran said it was the best in the country. Would
you get the glasses for me. They're in our so-called
kitchen—second shelf up on the right. (PAUL *exits to
the kitchen but is still visible to* JENNY.)

> (*There is a bustling on the stairs and* AUNT AGNES
> *appears at the open door. She is unable to see* PAUL
> *from her position just inside the door.*)

JENNY. Miss Nordstrom! Did you forget something?

> (PAUL *motions* JENNY *to say nothing about his
> presence.*)

AGNES. You just have to give me time to get my breath
again. Patricia will have to stay on the ground floor if
she expects many visits from me.

JENNY. Pat's not here. She and Fran went down for a
paper.

AGNES. No matter. (*still puffing*)

JENNY. Well, at least this gives me an opportunity to
apologize to you properly for the disastrous evening.

AGNES. It wasn't disastrous, my dear girl, and you needn't apologize. I may be a blundering old woman, but I'm not the fool Paul would have you believe.

JENNY. I don't understand.

AGNES. Paul put me in a cab—said he wanted his constitutional. Actually I supposed he was coming right back here. I'm surprised not to find him sampling Fran's sherry.

JENNY. (*glances quickly off to the kitchen and then laughs*) Won't you sit down?

AGNES. Not necessary. Won't stay a minute. At any rate, instead of calling you in the morning I decided to take care of the matter at once. I asked the driver to swing around the block and bring me back. I'll come right to the point. You will stay on here with the girls won't you?

JENNY. Of course. You weren't really upset then. Pat wanted so much to have your approval. She suspected you were a sort of sanctioning committee.

AGNES. Actually she was right, but I think you'll manage very well. The three of you. They do need you, you know.

JENNY. I'm beginning to think I need them. This may be

the closest to a home I've ever had. Home—a walk-up
on Christopher.

AGNES. Not so strange. I understand more than you realize, Jenny. I too lost a young man. Only it was a war
in my day—the second one back. John and I were going
to be married, but we hadn't counted on San Juan Hill.
They called that the bloodless war. Did you know that?

JENNY. Now it's my turn to be sorry. Max and I did have
a better deal, I guess. We were married—for two weeks.

AGNES. I guessed it was something like that. Only you
won't make the mistake I did. You don't have a family
watching you—making demands. And you do have the
girls.

JENNY. You're right. I do have the girls.

AGNES. Well, I'd better start down those stairs. I'd just as
soon Paul wouldn't find me gone when he gets to the
hotel. Good-bye, my dear. I'll see you again. Remember
you have an Aunt Agnes if you ever need one.

JENNY. I appreciate that. (*She kisses* AGNES *on the cheek
and* AGNES *exits.* PAUL *comes back into the room with
the glasses.*)

PAUL. Thanks for not exposing me. (*He is thoughtful.*)

JENNY. The bit about the sherry almost caught me off
guard.

PAUL. You know I felt like an eavesdropper. Would you believe I knew nothing about Agnes's John—or their plans?

JENNY. Pat said you were younger than . . .

PAUL. Not that much. I was twenty-one then. Not a child. But I was at college—miles away—wrapped up in my own affairs. And insensitive too, I suppose. But no one told me. She certainly never talked about it.

JENNY. I can understand that. What good. Could you have helped?

PAUL. I wonder if I would have tried. Dear old Aggie . . . all those years alone. (*He shakes his head in reflection.*) But Jenny, I think she was wrong, too. She should have talked about it. I don't think there's any wisdom in hiding the scars of our private lives.

JENNY. (*pours the sherry*) You are beginning to convince me that there isn't. Let's drink to that. And to something else—the future of the threesome on Christopher.

(*They lift their glasses as the curtain falls.*)

PRODUCTION NOTES

Greenwich Village in 1936 was an exciting place to live. The outlook was not as bleak as it was at the height of the Depression, and there was a promise in the air of better things. This lighthearted atmosphere should come across in *Walk-up on Christopher,* at least through Fran and Pat.

The set is a realistic one. The furniture and small props are not difficult to come by. Christmas cards and wrappings. A copy of *Gone With the Wind.* The coin cup. The picture on the mantle. Cups and saucers. Fran's suitcase under the daybed. The sherry bottle and the glasses. And do not forget the organ grinder music offstage.

Some of the dress is specified. Agnes has a hat and gloves, Paul an overcoat and muffler. Paul's hat isn't mentioned, but he would surely have one. For the rest, the library will provide books with verbal or actual pictures of what was in vogue.

The three girls are distinctly different. Pat, the youngest, is fresh from high school, exuberant, in love with life. Fran is dramatic, literary. Jenny is realistic, tolerant, considers herself removed from the fulfillment of dreams.

If it is desired, other events of 1936 could be woven into the dialogue. The King of England gave up his throne on December 11 of that year to marry Wally Simpson. The scrambled alphabet of President Roosevelt was always in the news—CCC, WPA, NRA. Take care, however, not to tip the scales with too much history. The play is not intended as a review of the year.

YOU HAVE TO STAY
ON THE HORSE

SUMMARY

Josie Harrigan, widowed on her honeymoon and a resentful mother at twenty, having left her son, Ted, to be raised by her older sister, Claire, returns at thirty-nine to claim him. She has become a successful fashion designer and wants Ted to go back with her to Paris at least for a year.

Ted refuses his mother's request, declaring that he has made plans which have priority, plans which include Aunt Claire, college, and a "special girl."

Confrontations between mother and son and between the sisters culminate in reproach and bitterness. In the end Josie leaves without telling her son the real reason for her plea.

YOU HAVE TO STAY ON THE HORSE

CHARACTERS

JOSIE TURNER HARRIGAN, 39, A DRESS DESIGNER OF SOME
    STATURE AND A SOPHISTICATE

CLAIRE TURNER, JOSIE'S SISTER AND HER SENIOR BY NINE
    YEARS. NOT MUCH STYLE BUT PLENTY OF WARMTH

TED HARRIGAN, JOSIE'S SON, 19, OUT OF HIGH SCHOOL A
    YEAR AND PLANNING ON COLLEGE IN THE FALL

GARFIELD TEWKS, ABOUT 70, FORMERLY THE OWNER OF A
    SMALL RIDING STABLE AT A MIDWESTERN LAKESIDE
    RESORT, HE IS NOW THE CARETAKER OF A NUMBER OF
    THE SUMMER COTTAGES, TURNER'S INCLUDED

DON PETERS AND HANK BENDER, FRIENDS OF TED

THE TIME: *Late afternoon a week before Memorial Day of the current year*

The scene is the living room of the Turner summer cottage. There are two doors on the right wall. The one downstage leads to the kitchen. The one upstage leads to the bedrooms. At the center back is a large bay window, and on the left wall downstage is the door to the outside. The furniture is adequate but somewhat outdated. A pair of well-used love seats face each other and flank the window. There is a coffee table, a couple of odd chairs and a desk, all arranged as desired. There is a clock (not electric) on the desk—or maybe on the wall— which has been allowed to run down. The resort community will come alive for the season with the Memorial

*Day weekend, but as yet the Turner cottage bears signs
of having been closed for the winter. The window shade
is drawn, there are no curtains, and the furniture is covered with sheets.*

As the curtain opens, JOSIE, *in a smart suit and groomed
to the fingertips, moves into the room from the outside
door. For a few moments she weighs and fingers the key
which has admitted her; then she places it on the coffee
table. She deposits her small overnight case on one of the
love seats and goes to the window to raise the shade. It
is a gloomy day but the room is lightened a little. Looking about her,* JOSIE *evaluates the place, remembering it,
and as she moves toward the door to the kitchen she is
startled by the voice of* GARFIELD TEWKS *who calls from
offstage left.*

GAR. Miss Claire! Ted! You in there? (*He knocks and then
fumbles with the door. Finding it open, he enters in
agitation. He is an old man, and his eyes aren't the
best. He squints at* JOSIE *who has turned when she
heard him.*) You ain't Miss Claire.

JOSIE. No. I'm not.

GAR. How'd you get in here? This is the Turner cottage,
and it was locked tighter than a stable door. I seen to
it myself.

JOSIE. (*recognizing him*) Gar! Gar Tewks! Don't you remember me? Josie—Josie Turner. Sure, the door was
locked all right. But the key was there in the little bird-

house—just where we always kept it. (*She indicates the key she has placed on the table.*)

GAR. (*in disbelief*) Josie? (*then not too cordially*) Well, I'm blamed if it ain't. Been a long time. Hear tell you're livin' off in some foreign country.

JOSIE. Paris. And I haven't been here at the cottage in almost twenty years. Not since my honeymoon.

GAR. Humph. (*He begins to take off the white coverings from the furniture.*)

JOSIE. (*more to herself than to* GAR) I used to wonder if things might have worked out if Eddie and I had had more time.

GAR. (*mumbling but distinctly audible*) Fightin'—always fightin'. I could hear ya way over at the stable.

JOSIE. Yeah. Ed was hot tempered. Still he wasn't a bad guy.

GAR. (*finally speaks directly to her*) Don't think much of a man can't sit astride a filly without gettin' hisself throwed—and killed into the bargain. He sure had no business at my stable. (*He points an accusing finger at* JOSIE *as though she is a child.*) And if you'd kept your bridegroom to home . . .

JOSIE. (*impatiently*) Oh, Gar, it's all done with. Let it rest. (*She changes the subject.*) The old place is sure quiet.

GAR. Folks'll be troopin' in soon. Won't be long. Had all the phones hooked up just this morning. And the lights and gas. Miss Claire never told me anybody'd be here today or I'd had the place aired.

JOSIE. She probably didn't have time. I called her just yesterday—caught a plane to New York, made good connections to Davenport, rented a car and here I am. Claire said they'd meet me—she and Ted. (JOSIE *looks at her watch and then goes to the window.*) I'd hoped to find better weather. It looks like it's going to rain any minute.

GAR. We're due for a good downpour, but that won't stop Miss Claire. If she said she'd come, she'll be here. And that goes for that boy of hers too.

JOSIE. (*catching the phrase "boy of hers"*) Ted, you mean? Ted's my boy, Gar. Have you forgotten that?

GAR. (*his hostility showing*) Ain't forgot you bore him. But ya ain't raised him. Far as I see he's Miss Claire's boy. (*There is a sound of car brakes offstage left.*)

CLAIRE. (*shouting just outside the door left*) Hello in there. (CLAIRE *enters. She is rather plain in a warm comfortable way and wears a trim shirtwaist dress and*

sweater. She deposits her purse on the nearest chair.)
Well, Josie. (*embraces her*) Do you realize we haven't
seen you for twelve years. How about that, Gar?
Twelve years. Let's have a look at you.

GAR. (*grumbling*) More years than that for me.

CLAIRE. (*holds* JOSIE *off at arm's length*) Well, my little
sister seems to be doing all right for herself. Fashions
by Josette. This a sample? (*She indicates Josie's suit.*)

JOSIE. Right off the drawing board.

GAR. (*interrupting*) Anything you want from the car, Miss
Claire?

CLAIRE. (*speaks as she inspects and admires Josie's outfit*) There are some groceries in the back seat, Gar.
Thanks. (*to* JOSIE) I like it. I'll bet it carries an expensive tag.

JOSIE. (*somewhat impatiently*) I do all right. I guess I
can't complain. Where's Ted?

CLAIRE. He should be here soon. (*She takes off her
sweater and tosses it over one of the chairs* GAR *has
uncovered.*) He had an appointment for a job over in
College View and he wasn't sure how long it would
take. One of his friends is bringing him up. I had told
you four o'clock so I wanted to get here. (*sets the clock*

by her watch and winds it as she speaks) Have you been waiting long?

JOSIE. Oh, no. Five minutes maybe. Did you say a job, Claire? Isn't Ted in school?

CLAIRE. Well, you know he graduated from high school last June. (*turns to face* JOSIE) We sent you an invitation. I hoped you'd come. (JOSIE *reacts and starts to say something but* GAR *comes in with the groceries and interrupts.*)

GAR. You want me to put these away?

CLAIRE. Just set the box in the kitchen, Gar. I'm really not sure whether we'll even stay over night. It looks pretty stormy.

GAR. (*heading for the kitchen*) The gas and lights is on. Did she tell you? (*He indicates* JOSIE *and exits without waiting for an answer.*)

CLAIRE. (*still talking to* JOSIE) Anyhow Ted's been working at the bank this year. Wasn't sure about college. But now he's decided. He's starting at the university this fall. He knew I wanted him to, but I think Marian had more to do with it than I did. She's probably why he's after this part time job, too. A little extra money. (CLAIRE *sits down on one of the love seats.*)

JOSIE. Marian?

CLAIRE. His very special girl.

JOSIE. It's hard to picture him old enough for a special girl.

CLAIRE. (*with a trace of bitterness*) I'm surprised you can picture him at all. You haven't seen him since he was seven.

JOSIE. Seven! Oh, Claire, that makes me so heartless. Sometimes I wish I could start over again.

GAR. (*This remark catches him on the way back from the kitchen.*) Can't do it—not after you've left the gate.

CLAIRE. What's that, Gar?

GAR. (*embarrassed*) Nothin', Miss Claire. Nothin'. If you want anything I'll be around. (GAR *exits mumbling to himself.*)

CLAIRE. I wonder what's the matter with him?

JOSIE. Oh, he's been upbraiding me. Gar never did like me much, even when I came here as a kid. You were always his favorite.

CLAIRE. Well, Josie, you weren't even born when Gar first opened the stable, and I practically lived over there. Loved the horses as much as he did. It was a shame

they made him close the place. It wasn't his fault Ed
had that accident.

JOSIE. According to Gar the whole thing was my fault.
Eddie and I had a real blow up that day. He was out
of his mind mad when he took that filly from her stall.
Of course he didn't have any business at the stable.
Gar's right about that. Ed didn't know one end of a
horse from the other.

> (*There is a bit of commotion offstage left.* CLAIRE
> *gets up and moves toward the outside door as*
> JOSIE *crosses to the right of the room, almost as
> though she is retreating.* TED *enters with his friends*
> DON *and* HANK *behind him. It has started to rain a
> little and they shake the moisture from their
> jackets.* TED *seems at ease, but underneath he is
> agitated.*)

TED. When that black cloud really decides to let go we'll
need a boat. You got here OK. (JOSIE *moves toward him
and starts to answer thinking he is speaking to her, but*
TED *walks to* CLAIRE *and addresses her directly.*) No
trouble?

CLAIRE. Of course not, Ted. You don't have to fuss over
me. (*She looks beyond* TED *to* HANK *and* DON.) Hi, fellows.

DON. Hi, Miss Turner. You look real well. You know Hank?

CLAIRE. (*crosses to greet them*) Of course I do. Good to see you.

TED. I sure didn't like the idea of you driving up here alone. I could just as well have taken the car and then gone back home to pick you up.

CLAIRE. No matter, and as it was Josie got here before I did. (*At the mention of* JOSIE, TED *becomes aware of her. She is still at the right side of the room.* CLAIRE *continues to talk.*) Oh, Hank, Don, this is Mrs. Harrigan, Ted's mother. (*There are acknowledgments all around.*)

TED. How about an introduction to me. Your son, Edward. Ted to my friends—and to relatives too, I guess.

JOSIE. I suppose I deserved that.

(*There is an embarrassing silence finally broken by* DON.)

DON. We have to run along. Just came in to say hello. Like Ted said, if that cloud really opens up we're in trouble.

CLAIRE. Oh, you can't leave right away. A few minutes more or less won't matter, Don. I stopped at the village and picked up something for sandwiches. Besides, I brought a cake, baked just this morning. I've never seen you refuse my chocolate cake.

DON. You've twisted my arm. (*He laughs.*) How about it, Hank?

HANK. You know I never turn down food.

CLAIRE. Come, on then. (*She starts for the kitchen but* TED *takes her arm.*)

TED. I'll feed them, Aunt Claire. You just take it easy. (TED *exits with* DON *and* HANK. *He is obviously eager to get away.*)

CLAIRE. I guess I am a little tired. (*She sits back on the love seat.*) I wonder if you'd hand me my purse, Josie. (JOSIE *does so and* CLAIRE *takes out a pillbox and puts a pill in her mouth.*)

JOSIE. (*pays no attention to the action*) He wasn't exactly overjoyed to see me.

CLAIRE. It has been twelve years, Josie. He doesn't know you. Twelve years, and those stingy little letters you write. Scarcely long enough to fold around the checks.

JOSIE. There were checks though. You'll have to give me credit for that.

CLAIRE. Oh you were generous with the money, but if only you could have spared a little time. Why couldn't you have taken him with you once in awhile. Poor Ted—

poor little guy. Boys should never be raised by maiden aunts. Even a widowed mother would be better.

JOSIE. I had to work, Claire—really work. Somebody had to make the money. And I did try to get you to bring him to me once—while I was still in New York.

CLAIRE. (*laughs*) You mean the year of the measles—the orthodontist—and the broken leg?

JOSIE. But I did ask for him. You talk as though I never had.

CLAIRE. We're splitting hairs, Josie. The point is Ted knew I wasn't his mother. He used to ask about you a good deal when he was small.

JOSIE. And then he stopped? Does he hate me that much?

CLAIRE. Josie, how can you hate someone you don't know. But he might have loved you if he'd had the chance. You could have married again, too, and given him a normal home.

JOSIE. I know what you're getting at—Mac.

CLAIRE. Well, you did tell me Mac would have been happy to have Ted.

JOSIE. (*angry*) Don't criticize me. I just couldn't settle for Mac. Bury myself way out there someplace in Texas.

I tried to get him to establish a business close to New York. I could have eased out of designing slowly. But he wouldn't do it. Mac was just too stubborn to see things my way.

CLAIRE. (*becoming exasperated and overwrought*) That's what you said when you came home that time, when Ted was seven. You only seem to need someone when there's a crisis. When Ed was killed. When you found out Ted was on the way. When you broke off with Mac. What is the crisis now?

JOSIE. Stop it, Claire. Stop it. You're tearing me apart. Don't do it.

CLAIRE. You mend easily, honey. Ted wasn't more than three months old when you packed off to design school on Ed's insurance money. And that other time, before Mac got across the wide Missouri on his way home, you opened up the Paris shop.

JOSIE. (*says nothing but walks to the window to look out*)

CLAIRE. We've been all around the bush, Josie. Why did you come here?

JOSIE. (*still at the window with her back to* CLAIRE) It was closer to the airport. You know how I dislike that home-town of ours.

CLAIRE. I mean why did you come at all?

JOSIE. (*turns and speaks abruptly*) All right, I'll tell you why I came. I want to take Ted back with me.

CLAIRE. To Paris?

JOSIE. Just for a year. Why not? He could go to school there just as well. You'll let him come, won't you?

CLAIRE. I don't write permission slips anymore. It's up to Ted.

JOSIE. It's terribly important to me . . .

(TED, DON, *and* HANK *reenter from the kitchen.*)

DON. Now that we've taken care of the food, we've just got to blast off, Miss Turner. You said it. I never could refuse your chocolate cake. Nice to meet you, Mrs. Harrigan. See you Ted.

HANK. I'll second that.

(*The boys exit.* CLAIRE *goes with them, and as* TED *starts to follow* JOSIE *stops him.*)

JOSIE. Stay here, Ted—please.

TED. (*shrugs and stays reluctantly, calling after* HANK *and* DON) Don—Hank—thanks again. I'll see you.

JOSIE. I know you don't remember much about me. I'm sorry.

TED. Should I remember? Let's see, what was I? Six—seven? Yes, there are a couple of things. Your long red fingernails and the perfume. It was terribly sweet. (*He looks at her critically.*) I'm not sure what I'm supposed to say. "Don't you think I've grown?" Or just simply, "So you're my mother."

JOSIE. That last has been established.

TED. Established but not discussed. You're a good looking mother . . .

JOSIE. You don't hate me, do you, Ted?

TED. I don't even know you.

JOSIE. Maybe we can change that.

TED. You mean you've come back to stay?

JOSIE. If I only could. I'm a working woman you know.

TED. Sure. Then why did you come? (*laughs*) To claim your child?

JOSIE. (*eagerly*) Could I?

TED. Forget it. You'd have to deal with Marian.

JOSIE. Marian's the special girl, I understand.

TED. That's right. We're getting married as soon as I'm through school. Sooner if I can swing it. Aunt Claire approves.

JOSIE. (*She has been somewhat reflective, but now she speaks with purpose.*) Ted, I want you to come back with me to Paris.

TED. You're putting me on.

JOSIE. Just for a year.

TED. I'm a working *man*. I got the job for fall.

JOSIE. You wouldn't have to take it. And you could go to school there maybe.

TED. (*laughs awkwardly*) So you really did come to claim me.

JOSIE. Just for a year. I do want you to know me, Ted, and I want to know you.

TED. Know me. Now that I'm all grown up and there's no danger of spilled milk or wet beds or nightmares. There are some memories of your visit I'd like to forget. You didn't want to know me then.

JOSIE. That's cruel, Ted. I was afraid of you when you

were small. Maybe all my mother instincts are descending on me now.

TED. Well it's just too late.

JOSIE. Is it? You and your Marian are young. (CLAIRE *re-enters but stands unnoticed inside the door.*) Your Aunt Claire thinks it's all right.

CLAIRE. I didn't say that, Josie. You twist people's words. I said it was up to Ted. He can go if he wants to.

TED. Well, I don't. And let's just not hear any more about it.

JOSIE. (*begins to wheedle*) It's such an opportunity. There's so much I could show you. So much to do. (*She puts her arms around Ted's waist.*) Paris is a beautiful city—but you could see the whole continent as well.

TED. (*pulls away from her*) I said I didn't want to hear any more about it. I've got my own plans.

JOSIE. Please, Ted. Please. I've come so far. I'm begging you. It means so much to me.

TED. (*moving toward the outside door*) You don't seem to understand. I can't.

JOSIE. You're not being fair. I've worked all my life for you. Don't you think you owe me something?

TED. (*turns on her, shouting in anger*) Owe you something. Well, I'm sure you've saved the canceled checks. I'll pay it back. All of it.

JOSIE. I don't want the money. I want you.

TED. God knows why. You've never given me any real thought before. And now you drop in out of the blue and expect me to be jazzed about going to Paris. Come on.

JOSIE. (*storming*) You're just like Ed—obstinate, unreasonable. You're like your father after all.

TED. OK, so I got something from both my parents. Only thing is the money I can give back—and don't think I won't. Even if it takes the rest of my life.

JOSIE. (*turns to* CLAIRE) You talk to him Claire.

CLAIRE. It's not my business, Josie. There's nothing I can say.

JOSIE. You've turned him against me.

CLAIRE. Josie, you know better than that.

TED (*furious that* JOSIE *is blaming* CLAIRE) You can't get it through your head that I don't want to go with you. I don't want to be with you. I don't want to know you.

I don't give a damn about Paris. I don't give a damn about . . .

(TED *doesn't finish the sentence. Instead he storms out the door left. Ever since Ted's arrival it has continued to rain and occasionally a crack of thunder has been heard in the distance. As* TED *exits there is a loud clap and a bright flash of lightning.*)

JOSIE. How can he say that? I was really counting on it.

CLAIRE. Were you, honestly? People make plans, Josie. Ted's no child. He has next year all laid out and the years to follow for that matter. He told you about Marian?

JOSIE. I still wouldn't think a year would be too much to ask. He has so much time. He's only nineteen.

CLAIRE. Do you remember when you were nineteen. You rushed headlong into that marriage with Ed. You didn't think there was time.

JOSIE. (*quietly*) You've made your point, Claire. (*She walks to the outside door left and stands with her back to* CLAIRE.) But I was right then without being aware of it. I don't have time.

CLAIRE. OK Josie, what's your real problem?

JOSIE. (*still without turning*) Claire, I'm going to die.

CLAIRE. What are you talking about?

JOSIE. (*turning*) Leukemia, Claire. I found out a year ago. (CLAIRE *reacts but does not speak.*) That's why I didn't come to Ted's graduation. Honestly that was the reason. I was in the hospital for tests. And I didn't come running—not right away. They said I had about three years, more or less. One of them's already gone.

CLAIRE. Oh, Josie.

JOSIE. (*She breaks down and runs to* CLAIRE.) Claire, Claire. I'm scared.

CLAIRE. (*with understanding*) Of course you wanted Ted for awhile. I can understand that.

JOSIE. It was foolish of me to think he'd come.

CLAIRE. You didn't tell him?

JOSIE. No. Oh, no.

CLAIRE. He'd probably go if you did. In fact I'm almost sure of it. I know Ted. He does have his whole life before him. You're right. One year isn't too much to ask of your own boy.

JOSIE. Gar said he was your boy, Claire, not mine. And he's right. (*At this moment* TED *comes back in. The storm has been rising all the time. It has grown darker and there is more thunder and lightning.*)

TED. (*He has obviously been running in the rain and is quite wet.*) I don't think we should stay here. The storm's getting worse. Gar says he doesn't know how long that road will be open.

CLAIRE. I suppose you're right. (*She is upset and confused over the knowledge she now has.*) Josie, you don't really have to hurry back. Maybe we won't let you go at all. You'll see. The old town might look pretty good.

JOSIE. Well . . . I guess I have no choice. I'd hate to be marooned here alone. (*hesitates*) I'm not sure I'm welcome though.

TED. Forget it. You probably own the house.

JOSIE. Would you ride back with me, Ted. Maybe I can . . .

TED. I'd just as soon Aunt Claire wouldn't tire herself out with so much driving in one day. You can follow us.

JOSIE. (*urgently*) I do have something to tell you . . .

CLAIRE. (*watching* TED *closely*) Go on with her, Ted. I can drive.

TED. Whatever she has on her mind can keep. It can't be that important after twelve years. Come on, Aunt Claire. I'd like to get over the bridge before dark.

CLAIRE. I won't bother carting that food stuff back to town. Let me tell Gar to take it.

TED. I'll see that he gets it. (*with affectionate authority*) You go get in the car. (*He gets Claire's sweater, helps her into it, and hustles her to the door.*)

CLAIRE. (*She breaks away from him for a moment and goes to* JOSIE.) You see how he orders me around, Josie. (*She tries to be flippant, takes* JOSIE *in her arms for a final hug.*) We'll see you later then. We've a lot of years to fill in. (*She exits and* TED *heads for the kitchen. When he returns with the box of groceries,* JOSIE, *who has been left alone for a moment, stops him with a hand on his arm.*)

JOSIE. Ted, there's a special reason for your coming to Paris.

TED. And there's a special reason why I can't. I wouldn't leave Aunt Claire. She's moving up to school with me next year. Didn't she tell you? (TED *sets the box down by the door.*)

JOSIE. (*surprised*) No, she didn't.

TED. I wouldn't go unless she'd do it that way. She hasn't been too well the last couple of years. Doc says it's her heart. And that old house is in a sad state of disrepair. She practically kills herself keeping it clean. We've already got a buyer for it and an apartment picked out up near the campus. Aunt Claire's excited about it.

JOSIE. But she was willing for you to come.

TED. Sure. That's Aunt Claire. I'm sorry I blew up, but like I said, it's just too late. And you acted like it was a matter of life and death.

JOSIE. (*grasping at straws*) You'd come if it were?

TED. (*laughing*) I suppose I'd have to. But with you looking like Ms. America that's a foolish "if." (JOSIE *starts to speak but hesitates and* TED *goes on.*) I'll tell you what. I'll take a rain check on that offer. In four years maybe you can broaden it to include a bride—OK?

JOSIE. Sure, Ted. I'll look forward to it.

(GAR *calls from offstage as he comes to the door.*)

GAR. Miss Claire says you're leaving. It's a good thing.

TED. Yes, and we'd better get going. By the way, Aunt Claire says you're to take this box of food. I'll just leave it here by the door. You can get it when you lock up for us. (*to* JOSIE) You know your way into town then, and we'll see you later.

JOSIE. I'll leave in a few minutes. (*She stands at the door as* TED *exits, then moves back into the room followed by* GAR.)

GAR. You about ready to go?

JOSIE. Just about. (*As though she has made a sudden decision, she turns abruptly to* GAR.) Do you know what I came back for? To take Ted to Paris with me. Since you despise me, you'll be glad to know he won't go.

GAR. I don't despise you, Miss Josie. I'm sorry for you.

JOSIE. He never called me "mother." Not once . . . not once . . .

GAR. You can't claim the purse, you know, 'less you stay on the horse.

JOSIE. (*She picks up her overnight case.*) I guess that's the way it is, but I had to try. You tell them that, Gar. You tell them just that, if they call up here after me. And tell them I'll wire them from New York and from Paris. And Gar . . . put the key back in the birdhouse. I'd like to know that it's there. (*She walks toward the door and then turns.*) I guess Eddie and I were two of a kind. Neither one of us stayed on the horse. (*She exits and* GAR *is left on stage. He draws the blinds at the window and shaking his head moves toward the door as the curtain closes.*)

PRODUCTION NOTES

The scene description in the script for *You Have to Stay on the Horse* is detailed and specific, but it lends

itself to change. If it is necessary to adjust to lesser facilities, the illusion of a door to be unlocked could be established. The bay window could be eliminated. Different
furniture could be used as long as it is appropriate for
a summer cottage.

This is a present-day drama. The costumes for Claire
and Josie can be other than those suggested if they are
in keeping with the characters and true to current styles.

The contrasts between Claire and Josie are obvious.
Ted might have a few mannerisms to set him apart from
his friends although his speeches define him quite well.
The other two boys should have certain attributes which
distinguish them from each other and from Ted. Hank,
who never turns down a chance to eat, might be on the
heavy side. Don would seem to be glib of tongue, at ease
with everyone. The young men are all nineteen, and their
clothes should be right for the time. Additions or changes
can always be made in dialogue to keep up with current
vernacular.

A check of the script will produce a list of hand props—
the clock, the box of groceries, Josie's overnight case, the
key.

The storm is important to the play. It is more than atmosphere. As it develops and intensifies it parallels the
same development and intensification of the conflict between the sisters and between Ted and his mother. Time
and effort should be given to the achievement of the
proper sound effects.

A ROLL OF NICKELS

SUMMARY

Pamela and Jeff Harding, returning from their honey-moon, make an unscheduled stop in Las Vegas. Among the guests of the hotel are Mrs. Murdick, a life-loving in-dividualist in her late seventies, her attractive and un-married daughter, Sylvia, and the Colonel, a robust, high-stake gambler from Montana.

Pamela's fear of gambling triggers a series of incidents which in turn brings into focus the multiple forces which shape people's lives.

A ROLL OF NICKELS

CHARACTERS

JEFF HARDING, A YOUNG LAWYER, NEWLY MARRIED

PAMELA HARDING, HIS BRIDE

MRS. MURDICK, A FREE SPIRIT IN THE PRIME OF HER LATE
SEVENTIES

SYLVIA MURDICK, HER DAUGHTER

THE COLONEL, A HIGH-STAKE GAMBLER AND A SOLID MAN

THE DESK CLERK

MR. STONE, A HOTEL GUEST

THE CASINO HOSTESS

THE GAMBLERS, AS MANY AS DESIRED

THE CROUPIER

THE BELLBOYS

THE TIME: *The present*

*The scene is laid in the lobby of one of the smaller hotels
in Las Vegas. The exit to the outside is downstage right,
and there is an exit upstage right which leads to a cocktail lounge, the coffee shop, and other facilities as well as
to the hotel rooms. The registration desk is along the right
wall, and at center back is a sofa flanked by lamp tables.
There are two lounge units at center stage which face
each other but are some distance apart. Each grouping
consists of a low table between two chairs placed at an
angle which allows the audience full view. There is no
defined wall on the left, and two gambling tables extend
out into the area of action bringing the casino into the*

lobby. The downstage table is for roulette and has a few high stools around it. The upstage table is for dice. The casino proper is offstage left. As the curtain rises, SYLVIA *and her mother enter from upstage right.* MRS. MURDICK, *a step or two ahead of her daughter, bustles in with a purpose. Her eyes are on the gambling tables and on the people gathered there.* SYLVIA *seems to be in no hurry and she carries a book.*

SYLVIA. Wait, Mama. Before we go into that casino, let's just sit here for awhile. (*She sits in the upstage lounge chair in the grouping at right center.*) It's so noisy in there.

MRS. MURDICK. (*who has come downstage intending to go off to the casino downstage left, now sits in the other chair in the same grouping*) Sylvia, you've done nothing but complain ever since we left home.

SYLVIA. You know I hate coming here, Mama. Just once I wish we could go someplace else when I have my vacation.

MRS. MURDICK. You are certainly your father's daughter. And how many times do I have to tell you? You don't need to come with me. I'd have more fun by myself anyhow.

(MR. STONE *enters from downstage right and comes to the desk to register.* MRS MURDICK, *who wants to see everything that goes on, turns around to take note of him.*)

SYLVIA. I couldn't let you traipse off to Las Vegas alone. You know I couldn't do that. How would it look?

MRS. MURDICK. It would look like an old lady was finally having herself a good time. The annuity your father left me had no strings to it. If I want to play a little black-jack that's my business. I'm not hurting anybody, and I'm well able to take care of myself.

(JEFF *and* PAMELA *enter from downstage right.* JEFF *carries a couple of pieces of luggage, and* PAMELA, *in sport clothes and with a colorful scarf around her head, moves into the lobby with a hesitancy which is obvious.*)

JEFF. (*puts the luggage down by the desk and takes off his sunglasses*) It's good to get out of the glare.

MRS. MURDICK. (*turns around again to see who spoke and then turns to* SYLVIA) That's a nice looking young couple. I'll bet they're newlyweds.

SYLVIA. (*with disinterest*) If they are, the bride doesn't look too happy.

PAMELA. (*standing a little behind* JEFF *at the desk*) It's only four o'clock, Jeff. We could have driven another hour or two.

JEFF. (*still waiting for the* DESK CLERK *to finish with* MR. STONE, *turns to* PAMELA) We're in no big rush, are we? Remember, as soon as we get home the honeymoon's over. Both of us have work to do. No more lazy days. Besides we couldn't go through Las Vegas without stopping. Where's your sporting blood?

PAMELA. (*reacts to the reference to gambling*) I've never gambled in my life. (*Then realizing she was sharp, she tries to cover up.*) As a matter of fact, I've never even been in Las Vegas before.

JEFF. (*with surprise*) You haven't? Then it's about time. Maybe we'll stay a couple of nights. You don't mind?

PAMELA. (*laughs a little uneasily*) It looks like you've already decided. But we didn't have a reservation. Are you sure we can get a room?

JEFF. I don't think that'll be a problem. Weren't you aware that you married a man of influence? (*He directs his attention to the desk and waits to be served.*)

(MRS. MURDICK *has gotten up and nonchalantly edged around behind her chair closer to the desk to listen to the conversation.*)

SYLVIA. (*whispers to her mother*) Mama, come back here.

(MRS. MURDICK *pays no attention to her.*)

DESK CLERK. (*finishes with* MR. STONE) Thank you, Mr. Stone. (*He rings for the* BELLBOY. MR. STONE *steps aside and the* CLERK *turns to* JEFF *who has taken out a credit card and laid it on the counter. In the meantime* MR. STONE *exits with the* BOY.)

JEFF. Do you suppose you could take care of a couple of tired and hungry people? (*As the* CLERK *proffers a registration form for* JEFF *to sign, he glances at the card.*)

CLERK. Certainly, Mr. Harding. Nice to have you with us. (*He looks at the registration which* JEFF *has now signed and then past* JEFF *to* PAMELA.) And Mrs. Harding. (*He rings the bell for another* BOY *and at the same time hands* JEFF *a small manila packet.*) Here's a little bonus from the house. Good luck now. (*As* JEFF *and* PAMELA *wait for a* BELLBOY *they move to upstage center crossing behind Sylvia's chair.*)

JEFF. Well, let's see what they're using for bait these days. (*He opens the envelope and takes out a batch of coupons.*)

PAMELA. He doesn't need to wish me good luck.

JEFF. (*thumbing through the coupons*) Hmm, complimentary coffee in the morning . . . free cocktails . . . and how about this . . . a ticket redeemable for a roll of nickels. (*He pockets the coupons.*) Shall we wander into the casino and look around before we go to our room? The boy can go on with the bags and bring us the key. Are you hungry?

PAMELA. Not too. And I would like to go to the room first.

JEFF. Fine. There's no hurry. No hurry at all. Time hangs in limbo here. (*to the* BELLBOY *who is now waiting for them*) OK, lead the way. (*The three exit upstage right.*)

SYLVIA. Mama, you shouldn't listen in on other people's conversation.

MRS. MURDICK. (*comes around behind Sylvia's chair to upstage center and turns to face her daughter*) I like people. You know you have an amazing facility for taking the light out of life. (*She moves to left stage with this last line and looks off into the casino.*) There's the colonel, that nice officer we met last year. (*She waves.*) He said he usually comes for the whole summer. I'd hoped he would be here. I have always leaned toward military men.

SYLVIA. Mama, he's no colonel. They just call him that.

MRS. MURDICK. You are such a skeptic, Sylvia. And actually I think he was interested in you.

SYLVIA. Mama, you've been pushing me at men for twenty-five years. I wish you'd stop it.

MRS. MURDICK. You certainly don't cooperate. You gave the colonel absolutely no encouragement.

SYLVIA. There was nothing to encourage. He was just being friendly.

MRS. MURDICK. You have to meet a man halfway, Sylvia. Play your cards right.

SYLVIA. Besides, he's a big time gambler. I've watched him. He thinks nothing of letting thousands of dollars ride on a throw of the dice. How could he possibly be interested in someone like me?

MRS. MURDICK. (*with a sigh*) You have no self-confidence. It's no wonder you've been buried all these years in the archives of that art museum.

SYLVIA. I've never complained about my life and the way I live it. (*The* COLONEL, *who has seen the* MURDICKS, *enters from the casino and comes to greet them, especially* SYLVIA.)

THE COLONEL. Well, if it isn't the little ladies from California.

MRS. MURDICK. Colonel, how good to see you. Sylvia was just saying she hoped you would be here.

(SYLVIA *gives her mother a barbed look.*)

THE COLONEL. I'm glad to see a couple of familiar faces myself. They've got so many new people out there on the floor—on both sides of the tables. I don't rightly feel at home. How've you been doing?

MRS. MURDICK. Just got in this morning. Haven't had time to get warmed up yet. Sylvia is always my good luck and I have to wait until she's ready. I always say get a nongambler to stand beside you and fortune smiles.

THE COLONEL. I could use a little luck. (*leans invitingly toward* SYLVIA) Will you oblige?

MRS. MURDICK. Why don't you two run along? Have a go at it.

SYLVIA. No thanks. You can go if you want to, Mama. I'll wait here.

MRS. MURDICK. (*with disappointment*) I guess we're not quite ready, Colonel. Later perhaps.

THE COLONEL. Whatever you say. As a matter of fact I've a couple of phone calls to make. Why don't I pick you up on my way back?

(*He exits upstage right.*)

SYLVIA. Mama, must you always embarrass me?

MRS. MURDICK. Nonsense. He likes you. And surely you will admit that he is a very attractive man.

SYLVIA. If it makes you feel any better I admit that. And he is also pleasant. I like him.

MRS. MURDICK. Well then, don't be a shrinking violet.

> (JEFF *and* PAMELA *reenter from upstage right. They are wearing the same clothes.* PAMELA *has simply taken the scarf from her head and changed shoes. She clings to Jeff's arm.*)

MRS. MURDICK. There's the young couple again. They didn't take long.

> (SYLVIA *has opened her book and ignores her mother's remark.* PAMELA *and* JEFF *come downstage right past the desk, and the* HOSTESS *who has been milling around the roulette table comes to meet them.*)

HOSTESS. Good evening. Or I guess it's still afternoon, isn't it? (*laughs*)

JEFF. It doesn't seem to matter here. And so far it's fine. (*He takes the coupon from his pocket.*) How about this roll of nickels?

HOSTESS. Our pleasure. (*She takes the coupon* JEFF *holds*

out and gives PAMELA *a roll of coins.*) But this should
go to the lady.

JEFF. Fair enough. My wife can't wait to break the house
with its own money.

PAMELA. He's joking. I'm no gambler.

JEFF. (*laughs*) I don't think it takes a gambler to pull
the handles on those lemon machines. (*They move
away from the* HOSTESS.) OK, get out the nickels. With
beginner's luck, who knows? You may win enough to
pay for our dinner.

PAMELA. (*holds the roll out to him*) You take them, Jeff.

JEFF. No. They were given to you. Here. (*He tears open
the packet and shakes the shiny coins out into the palm
of her hand.*)

PAMELA. (*starts to open her purse*) Then I'll just keep
them.

JEFF. (*in mock dismay*) You wouldn't! You know that
wasn't the idea.

PAMELA. You said they were given to me. I don't want to
gamble, Jeff. I can't.

JEFF. Why not?

PAMELA. It's just a thing with me.

JEFF. You're missing all the fun. Besides you aren't really putting up any money. They weren't your nickels in the first place. Come on.

> (*With* JEFF *pulling* PAMELA *by the hand they exit downstage left into the casino where the slot machines are.*)

MRS. MURDICK. (*who has been listening, speaks as she follows the young couple to the exit*) I've got to watch this.

SYLVIA. (*looks up from her reading*) Mama. I don't think it's any of your business.

MRS. MURDICK. (*ignoring the admonition, keeps her attention on what is happening offstage*) I've never seen anybody so nervous over a slot machine.

SYLVIA. I can understand how she feels. She just finds no joy in it.

MRS. MURDICK. (*still watching*) And nickels! You'd think she had a million riding on the pull of that handle . . . Saints alive! She hit the jackpot. They're coming back. (*She retreats from her observation point, moving quickly to the far right and then around to stand behind* SYLVIA. *She is a bit breathless as* JEFF *reenters with* PAMELA, *obviously shaken, following behind him.*)

SYLVIA. (*Looking up briefly, she speaks to* MRS. MURDICK.) You'll get caught doing that some time.

JEFF. (*He had put the jackpot nickels in his pocket and now he transfers them to the table between the two chairs at left center.*) There now, that didn't hurt, did it? And what did I tell you. (*He counts out the coins as he talks.*) Beginner's luck.

MRS. MURDICK. (*to* SYLVIA) That girl has some kind of a problem.

SYLVIA. Well, you just stay out of it, Mama.

JEFF. (*who has finished counting*) Not bad. Now we'll get you some dollars and you can try the . . .

PAMELA. (*without turning toward him*) Please, Jeff. I don't want to.

JEFF. You can't break a lucky streak. (*He has scooped up the nickels again and dumped them back in his pocket.*) Let's go.

PAMELA. No! (*Her voice rises to a high pitch.*) Let me alone.

JEFF. OK. Play it soft. Somebody might think we're married. (*He laughs uneasily.*)

PAMELA. (*turns toward him*) I'm sorry, Jeff.

JEFF. (*gently*) What's wrong with you, Pam?

PAMELA. (*sits on the downstage chair of the left center grouping and speaks with indecision*) Jeff, there's never been any reason for me to tell you, but my father was a gambler.

JEFF. (*who stands beside the chair*) So. Isn't everybody? One way or another?

PAMELA. His gambling was a problem. Sometimes his paycheck didn't get past the bookie's corner. When I was little that's all I heard. *Your father is a gambler . . . and that is bad. You must never be like him.*

JEFF. Your mother got to you, that's for sure.

PAMELA. Oh, no, not my mother. She loved him. No, it was grandpa who pounded at me about gambling. I think he hated my father. You know one day when I was about seven he found me matching pennies with the little girl next door. "I might have known," he said. "You have your father's blood." I can still hear his voice and feel the sting of his knuckles across my hand. (*She opens her hand almost as though she expected the pennies to roll out.*)

JEFF. Ridiculous, honey. This is just an obsession. And now is the time to get rid of it. Come on, I'll hold your hand. (*He pulls her gently to her feet, and still in a kind of daze she goes with him to the casino again.*)

MRS. MURDICK. (*who has taken in the whole scene*) That poor little girl is frightened to death. (*She walks to the left exit again to watch* JEFF *and* PAMELA *and their activity offstage.*)

SYLVIA. (*for the most part occupies herself with her book*) I still say it's none of your business, Mama.

MRS. MURDICK. (*reporting the action taking place offstage*) He *is* holding her hand. She's playing with dollars now. (*She shakes her head, clucks her tongue, as the dollars are obviously gobbled up by the machine. Then she shouts with excitement.*) What do you know about that! Another jackpot! But she's certainly not very excited about it. (MRS. MURDICK *retreats again, this time to stand downstage at the far right as* PAMELA, *emotionally upset, hurries in from the casino.* JEFF, *in high spirits, follows her.*)

JEFF. Didn't I tell you? You are hot, Mrs. Harding. Let's see what you got this time. (*He goes between the two chairs at left stage and sits in the one upstage to count out the dollars.*)

PAMELA. (*Stands for a minute at center stage with her eyes closed. Then she sinks into the downstage chair at left center.*) You just don't understand, Jeff. It makes me ill . . . really ill.

JEFF. (*leans over the table toward her*) That's crazy.

Don't you trust me? Do you think I'd let you do anything that would hurt you?

PAMELA. (*softly*) I love you, Jeff. And I feel safe with you, but . . .

JEFF. Let's go then. This time we'll try roulette.

PAMELA. Please don't ask me to. I can't. I just can't.

JEFF. (*realizing that they are both tired*) Sure, honey. Maybe we should have dinner anyhow. I could use some food. Do you want to come with me to see when they can take us? We might have to wait a bit.

PAMELA. No, you go. I'll stay here.

JEFF. (*taking her hands in his*) You sure you'll be all right?

PAMELA. Sure.

JEFF. OK. (*He gets up, looks at her with loving concern, and heads downstage left to go to the dining room which is on the other side of the casino. After a few steps he turns to reassure her and himself.*) I'll be right back. (*He exits.*) (MRS. MURDICK *has been listening closely and now goes to* PAMELA.)

MRS. MURDICK. I couldn't help watching you. I've never seen anyone upset about winning before.

(PAMELA *turns her head away and bites her lip.*)

SYLVIA. (*who has been sitting in the upstage chair of the right grouping all this time under cover of her book*) Mama, don't bother her.

MRS. MURDICK. You just stay where you are, Sylvia. I don't need your advice. (SYLVIA, *in irritation, gets up and moves to the sofa at the back and resumes her reading while* MRS. MURDICK *speaks again to* PAMELA.) My daughter thinks I'm a busybody. Her father was a good solid man and I loved him, but I wish we could have produced a child with more imagination, more sense of adventure. (PAMELA *keeps looking away and* MRS. MURDICK *seats herself in the upstage chair beside her.*) You don't have to talk to me, child. I'll do the talking. That's one advantage of being over seventy-five. People tolerate you. They may think you a nuisance, but they aren't apt to call the security guard. Didn't I hear you say you hadn't been to Las Vegas before? Exciting place. I love it. Flashy and a lot of sham, but exciting. And I like games of chance. Some people like fishing. Some like baseball. Some just like to sit and watch television. I happen to like blackjack. I come here for two weeks each summer. I know how much I can spend on a vacation and I choose to spend it here. Once in awhile I win, but mostly I go home with nothing but the knowledge that I've had a good time. And I've lost only what I could afford, no cause for tears. Oh, I've seen people cry over their losses . . . But no, I don't believe I've ever seen anybody cry when he won.

PAMELA. (*looks around apparently hoping* JEFF *will come back*) I didn't mean to create a scene. I'm sorry.

MRS. MURDICK. A scene! In Las Vegas! Only a nosy old woman would notice. And I'm afraid I notice everything. (*takes the opportunity to reach* PAMELA) That lovely wedding ring of yours, for example. It's beautiful.

PAMELA. (*with the spontaneous pride of the bride*) Thank you. Jeff picked it out. I didn't even see it until he put it on my finger. He has good taste.

MRS. MURDICK. Obviously. You are very pretty.

PAMELA. (*embarrassed*) I didn't mean that.

MRS. MURDICK. True though. (*She extends her left hand to display a simple gold band.*) I had to pick out my own ring. Sylvia's father was rather prosaic, I'm afraid.

PAMELA. Did you and your husband come here together?

MRS. MURDICK. Oh, my no. He didn't like bright lights and crowds. His idea of a vacation was a tour of Wall Street. And he was pretty straitlaced. Maybe a bit like your grandfather. You see I did listen.

(PAMELA *turns away again but* MRS. MURDICK *puts a comforting hand on her arm as the* COLONEL *enters from upstage right and goes directly to* SYLVIA.)

THE COLONEL. Promised to be back and here I am. (*sits beside her*)

SYLVIA. Mama's found someone to mother. I think she's given up on me. She means well, but . . .

THE COLONEL. Your mother is an interesting woman. Seems to run in the family.

SYLVIA. You say all the gracious things, but I think a man like you must find me inordinately dull.

THE COLONEL. We don't see ourselves as others see us.

SYLVIA. You know I'm not a gambler. Couldn't be if I wanted to. I stay out of the casino as much as possible.

THE COLONEL. (*laughs*) I know. I remember from last year. You used to escape whenever you could. And usually behind a book.

SYLVIA. I just haven't the stamina for it. Everything moves so fast in there. I can't keep up with it.

THE COLONEL. That doesn't surprise me. But one thing does—did—that you hoped I'd be here.

SYLVIA. I didn't say that. Mama did.

THE COLONEL. I was afraid that might be the fact. No

matter. Maybe you would stand beside me anyhow.
Give me that good luck.

SYLVIA. Mama wasn't telling the truth about that either.
I'm not anybody's good luck, I'm afraid.

THE COLONEL. Don't be too sure. I agree with your mother
that a nongambler at your side is a good thing. It's one
of my particular superstitions. You know I don't often
cultivate people here. It's best that way in this mecca
of misfortune. But I like stimulating company when
I can get it. Your mother is occupied. Would you have
a cocktail with me? We might find it interesting to take
stock of our differences. (*He stands and offers his hand
to her.*)

SYLVIA. (*with sincerity*) Thank you. I'd like that. (*She
takes his hand and rises.*) I'll tell mama where we'll be.
(*She starts to move toward her mother but he stops
her.*)

THE COLONEL. She'll know you're not far away. And I
have a feeling she would approve of our talking together.

SYLVIA. You are so right . . . (*She hesitates and then
finishes her sentence with a smile.*) . . . Colonel. (*They
start toward the exit upstage right.*) I am not really
the antagonist I seem to be with mama. I am just direct
and realistic. Forgive me for that. I must be honest,

though. It *was* mama who said she hoped you'd be here this year, but I was indeed thinking it.

THE COLONEL. Good girl. (*He squeezes her arm and they exit.*)

(MRS. MURDICK, *who has been whispering consolations to* PAMELA *while the* COLONEL *and* SYLVIA *talked, has nonetheless been aware of their encounter. Now she turns all her attention to the troubled girl.*)

MRS. MURDICK. I know you wish your husband would come back and rescue you. Go ahead and say it. I understand.

PAMELA. I was wondering what was taking him so long.

MRS. MURDICK. There must have been a crowd waiting. Sylvia and I usually hold off till quite late for dinner. After the rush. Except tonight, God willing, I may dine alone. Sylvia also thinks I'm a matchmaker, but the colonel is good for her. I feel it. A direct opposite. Sometimes I think that's why I had a good marriage. Maybe if I had had a man like . . .

PAMELA. My father?

MRS. MURDICK. Well, yes. Two of a kind might have been a disaster.

PAMELA. (*in defense*) There were some very wonderful things about my father. I didn't have him long, but I remember what a gentle man he was.

MRS. MURDICK. I can see you loved him.

PAMELA. Oh, yes, I was on my mother's side. I adored him. When he tucked me into bed he used to sing some crazy song about a bullfrog, and sometimes he stayed until I fell asleep. I felt so safe with him. It was like being backed up to a mountain so that nothing could get at me from behind.

MRS. MURDICK. Your memories sound fine.

PAMELA. There just weren't enough of them. It all ended when I was eight. Mother had gone to the track with him. One of those rare times. I often wondered what kind of a day they had together. There was an accident on the way home. They were both killed. I was raised by my grandparents . . . (*She stops abruptly.*) I don't know why I'm telling you this.

MRS. MURDICK. Sometimes a stranger is the best person to confide in. But haven't you ever told your husband?

PAMELA. It was all so long ago. Grandpa died when I was fifteen. By the time I met Jeff it was far behind me. It was this place that brought it back. Grandpa blamed my father for my mother's death, and he used to say, "Remember, gambling brought about the loss of your mother. You must never gamble. Never. One time and you are in trouble."

MRS. MURDICK. You don't really believe that?

PAMELA. I never even buy a raffle ticket.

MRS. MURDICK. But we all gamble every day of our lives. Your mother took a chance when she married your father, but she loved him. Sometimes we love people because of their imperfections. You're taking a chance with your husband, too.

PAMELA. But Jeff's so solid. He's already a junior partner in a well-known law firm. Even grandpa would have approved.

MRS. MURDICK. Are you really afraid you have inherited your father's weakness?

PAMELA. I don't know . . .

MRS. MURDICK. Maybe it will be a heritage from your mother which will shape your life. There's a fifty-fifty chance of that. There! You see, chance again.

PAMELA. (*with a bit of a laugh*) I guess you're right. (*She sees* JEFF *entering downstage left and gets to her feet.*)

JEFF. (*hurrying over to* PAMELA) I'm sorry to have been so long. They had a big convention party lined up at the reservation desk and the maître d' was a new man.

PAMELA. Did you get a table?

JEFF. We'll still have to wait a bit. They'll call us.

MRS. MURDICK. They're always busy in the dining room this time of the year, but the food is good. I've just been chatting with your wife.

PAMELA. Oh, I'm sorry. Jeff, this is . . . why, I don't even know your name.

MRS. MURDICK. (*with a laugh*) Smith-Brown-Jones. Names aren't too important here.

JEFF. (*laughs in return*) Well, I'm glad to know you, Mrs. Smith-Brown-Jones. Thanks for keeping my wife happy.

MRS. MURDICK. I hope I did. Now I'm off to the casino. See you later. And good luck. (*She exits upstage left.*)

JEFF. The lady must have been good for you. And since you're in such fine spirits, let me show you the roulette table while we wait.

> (JEFF *sweeps* PAMELA *off to the roulette table upstage left and sees that she is seated on one of the end stools.* PAMELA *closes her eyes, shudders, and hugs her arms.*)

JEFF. Are you cold? Want a sweater? I think you left it in

the car. I'll get it. (*to the* CROUPIER) Give her a stack of chips. I'll be right back. (*He exits downstage right.*)

THE CROUPIER. (*who is at Pamela's left on the upstage side of the table puts a stack of chips in front of her and then begins his usual patter*) Place your bets, ladies and gentlemen. Place your bets. (*The* GAMBLERS *around the table respond, the wheel is spun and the chips are swept away.*)

ONE GAMBLER. (*leans over to* PAMELA) Aren't you going to play, sweetie?

(PAMELA *closes her eyes and with trembling fingers shoves a stack of chips out onto a number. Once again there is the spin of the wheel, the croupier's patter, and the chips are swept away.*)

ANOTHER GAMBLER. (*slides off his stool and moves away*) Easy come, easy go.

THE CROUPIER. Here we go again folks. On the red there. On the black. (*to* PAMELA) How about it, young lady?

(PAMELA *pushes the rest of her chips onto the board with no interest in where they rest.*)

THE CROUPIER. The young lady puts her chips on the black. OK. Here we go.

A THIRD GAMBLER. Without even looking. Now there's a gambler!

> (*Instinctively* PAMELA *reacts to the word gambler as the wheel is spun again. She looks furtively around the lounge area and the lobby. The wheel stops.*)

THE CROUPIER. Red wins, folks. Red is the winner.

> (*Just at this moment the* COLONEL *and* SYLVIA *enter from upstage right.* PAMELA *slides from the stool and runs blindly toward the* COLONEL.)

PAMELA. (*throwing herself into his arms*) I won't do it again, Grandpa. I won't do it again.

THE COLONEL. Well, well, little girl. What's the trouble now? (*The* COLONEL *puts his arm around* PAMELA *and with* SYLVIA *by his side they bring her back to one of the chairs at center stage.*) You sit right here. Everything's all right. (*to* SYLVIA) Do you know who she is, who she belongs to?

SYLVIA. It's the bride, the girl mama was talking to. I don't know her name. They checked in just this afternoon. Her husband's around somewhere. Oh yes, he went in to make a dinner reservation, I think. That's when mama started talking to her.

THE COLONEL. Maybe he's still in the dining room.

SYLVIA. It was an awfully long time ago.

THE COLONEL. You stay with her. I'll see if I can find him.

SYLVIA. (*calls to him as he heads for the exit*) Nice looking fellow. Light blue sports jacket. (*The* COLONEL *exits
downstage left without noticing that* JEFF *has entered
downstage right with Pamela's sweater over his arm.*
JEFF *spots* PAMELA *and hurries to her.*)

SYLVIA. (*looks up to see him*) Oh, there you are.

JEFF. Pamela, what's the matter?

PAMELA. I'm OK.

SYLVIA. Your wife was a little upset, but I think she's all
right now that you're here.

JEFF. What happened?

PAMELA. Nothing . . . nothing. I'm sorry to cause so much
trouble.

JEFF. Forget it. I'd just like to know what upset you.

PAMELA. I'll tell you on the way home, Jeff. And I do
want to go home. Could we?

JEFF. Sure. First thing in the morning if it's that important.

PAMELA. Couldn't we go now?

JEFF. I don't think either one of us is up to driving all night, Pam.

PAMELA. You're right, of course. I'll just go take a couple of aspirin and get some sleep.

JEFF. Don't you want to eat something? We ought to be able to get in the dining room by now. If not we'll go to the coffee shop.

PAMELA. I'm really not hungry, Jeff. And I don't think I could eat.

JEFF. Whatever you say. Come on.

PAMELA. You don't have to come with me. I'll be all right, and you're hungry.

JEFF. Don't worry about me. I'll have some dinner. I'll get you settled in first. Then I'll come back.

(*They exit upstage right as the* COLONEL *reenters from the casino.*)

THE COLONEL. He's not at the dining room.

SYLVIA. He found her. Came in right after you left. She seems to have some kind of a problem about Las Vegas —or about gambling, I guess.

THE COLONEL. I didn't quite understand it all. I'm not sure I liked the idea of being mistaken for anybody's grandpa, though. (*laughs*) Didn't realize I was aging so rapidly.

SYLVIA. (*laughs also*) Well, she seemed to be talking out of childhood memory. And you know the "anybody over thirty" bit.

THE COLONEL. (*thoughtfully*) I don't think I'd ever want to be under thirty again.

SYLVIA. Anyhow the young man seemed to have the right answers. She'll be all right. (*looks around*) Mama must have gone to the casino.

THE COLONEL. Yes. I saw. She was beaming.

SYLVIA. I'm sure of it. All that talk of her needing me by her side is nonsense. She'd rather I stayed home, you know. (MRS. MURDICK *hurries in from the casino.*)

MRS. MURDICK. I'm glad to find you two.

THE COLONEL. Well, you missed the excitement.

MRS. MURDICK. What happened?

SYLVIA. It was the bride. Not important now. The groom has taken over. You don't need to worry about her.

THE COLONEL. Look, I've convinced your daughter the three of us should have dinner together. And afterward she's promised to give me that luck of hers at the dice table.

MRS. MURDICK. That's what I came in to tell you. Don't count on me. I've got someone holding my spot and have to get back. Things are looking up, and I have a feeling this is my lucky night.

THE COLONEL. Whatever you say.

> (JEFF *reenters. He has come to get Pamela's sweater which he had left on the chair.* SYLVIA *sees him first and makes a move toward him.*)

SYLVIA. How is she? OK?

> (*Before* JEFF *has a chance to answer, the* COLONEL *sees him.*)

THE COLONEL. Jeff! Jeff Harding. Where in the world have you been keeping yourself the last eight months. Nobody told me you were here. But then they've got a whole new crew. How's the law game?

JEFF. Colonel! You son-of-a-gun. It has been a long time.

SYLVIA. I was just going to say, Colonel. This is the groom.

THE COLONEL. The groom! So that's what you've been up to. Got yourself a wife. (*It dawns on him that* JEFF *is*

the husband of the troubled bride.) The groom! Say
I've met the little filly. She's a bit skittish but she's a
beauty.

JEFF. Easily gentled though.

THE COLONEL. Well, you young rascal. How's about it.
Ed's in town from Philadelphia, and Ben Hagen and
Fred Mills. Let's even the old score. Say about eleven
in my room?

JEFF. Yes. Yes, I think I can make it.

THE COLONEL. Fine. What's the ante now? Where did we
leave it?

JEFF. Let's see. Two thousand, I think, Colonel. At least
that'll do for a starter.

(MRS. MURDICK *reacts to this, and* SYLVIA *touches
her arm and shakes her head as the curtain falls.*)

PRODUCTION NOTES

In *A Roll of Nickels* the atmosphere of a Las Vegas
casino can be caught and maintained if there are people
milling about and if there is muffled conversation and
laughter, all kept at low key and in the background.
Nothing should interfere with essential action or dialogue
of the play.

The Colonel is a rancher and an outdoorsman, and his
manner should reflect such a personality. He would prob-

ably wear boots and a western jacket because he obviously has money enough to do as he pleases. He is also a polished man of the world, however, and could be more elegantly dressed if that is desired.

The only specifications for Pamela are the scarf, the change of shoes, a purse. For Jeff there are the sunglasses and the blue sport coat mentioned by Sylvia when she sends the Colonel to find "the groom."

Sylvia will be smartly dressed in contemporary fashion. Mrs. Murdick will certainly match her daughter in attractive and appropriate apparel. She is no dowdy old lady and will wear makeup and jewelry with the same flair she brings to her holiday.

There are only a few small props to remember. Sylvia's book, the sweater that Pamela has left in the car, the chips, dice and other accouterments for the gambling tables, and whatever is needed for the reservation desk. There will be luggage for Jeff and Pamela as well as for Mr. Stone, who is the only incidental character mentioned by name.

The realism of walls and doors for the set of this play is optional. It is more important to create the feeling that this is indeed a Las Vegas hotel and that off through the left exits the gambling casino proper is crowded and buzzing with activity.

THE LAST BUS FROM LOCKERBEE

SUMMARY

One ordinary day, shortly before Christmas, John Gresham, a retired professor, makes his way to the bus station. He knows neither which bus nor whom he has come to meet. In the late afternoon he is joined by a young woman who, unlike him, knows exactly for whom she is waiting, but she is shrouded in a fog.

The ensuing interaction prepares the audience for a bus no longer in service, for people no longer alive, for an enigmatic child, but not for the sadness of what might have been.

THE LAST BUS FROM LOCKERBEE

CHARACTERS

JOHN GRESHAM, A RETIRED PROFESSOR, ABOUT 70

NED BARRETT, SENIOR TICKET AGENT, FARLAND BUS LINES

CHRIS ALLEN, COLLEGE STUDENT, NIGHT SHIFT TICKET
  AGENT

THE YOUNG WOMAN, DOLORES

MRS. HOFFMAN, THE SUPERVISOR AT BRIARWOOD

EUGENE GRESHAM, JOHN GRESHAM'S SON

BUS DRIVER, OFFSTAGE VOICE

ESTHER GRESHAM, JOHN GRESHAM'S WIFE

THE LITTLE GIRL

BUS PASSENGERS, AS MANY AS NEEDED AND DESIRED

THE MAN WHO COMES IN FROM THE STREET

THE TIME: *Late afternoon one day midweek before the
Christmas holidays of the present year*

*The scene is laid in the bus station of a small city. At
center back is a long ticket counter with a latched gate
opening at the left end of it. On the right side of the
counter there is a door to the rest rooms. The exit at left
stage leads to the street through wide double doors. The
right exit, with similar doors, opens out to the area where
the bus passengers are unloaded. There are a couple of
standard waiting room benches, one at left center and
one at right center, parallel to the footlights and facing
the audience. Several trash containers, stand-up ash trays
and anything else that is desired which fits into a bus*

station setting are placed in appropriate spots. A Christ-
mas wreath or two and a few strings of tinsel provide a
meager recognition of the season.

When the curtain opens, JOHN GRESHAM *is seated at*
the far right of the bench at right center. He is well
dressed, a gentleman with dignity and bearing. In the
buttonhole of his overcoat is a white flower and his hat,
which he has removed, is on the bench beside him. He
has a bus schedule in hand, and as he pores over it he
rubs his eyes and forehead in a gesture of perplexity.
NED BARRETT, *the senior ticket agent, is behind the counter*
preparing to end his shift. CHRIS ALLEN, *the night man,*
enters from the left.

CHRIS. (*looks at his watch and speaks with the exuberance
of youth*) Second day on the job, and I'm still getting
here on time.

NED. (*with jovial sarcasm*) Hallelujah! I don't suppose it
occurred to you that you might even come a little early.

CHRIS. (*laughs*) I don't want to overdo it, Mr. Barrett. Got
to take one step at a time.

NED. That's the trouble with you college fellows. You're so
busy changing the world, you can't allow a few extra
minutes for changing shifts.

CHRIS. (*suddenly serious*) It's not really the whole world
I want to change, Mr. Barrett. Just one facet of it. I sure

hope I can help people some day. And I'm glad to have this job. You know that. Any excitement?

NED. Naw. Couple of punks came in looking for trouble, but I got rid of them. Still pretty slow today. We won't have much holiday travel until the end of the week. It gave me a chance to clear up some book work.

    (CHRIS *removes his windbreaker and his knitted cap and prepares to take over his shift as he speaks.*)

CHRIS. I'd just as soon have it slow too. I've got a term paper to write. (*he indicates* GRESHAM.) Who's the old dude with the flower in his buttonhole? Pretty classy for a bus station.

NED. I don't know him. To tell you the truth it's the first time I've ever seen him in here.

CHRIS. Maybe he's going someplace.

NED. If he is he hasn't made up his mind where. He came in this morning before nine o'clock and he's been here ever since. He's been acting kind of strange, too. And come to think of it, he didn't even go anyplace for lunch. Hmmm.

CHRIS. Maybe he's meeting somebody?

NED. Coming in at nine and waiting around all day wouldn't make any sense on that score either. Anyhow he didn't ask any questions. I just let him alone. He isn't bothering anybody. (*During this speech* NED *has taken his coat and cap from the rack. As he starts to come out from behind the counter the phone rings and he steps back to answer it.*)

NED. (*into the phone*) Farland Bus Lines. Ned Barrett speaking. Yes? Mrs. Wilson? Oh, yes. An old guy? White hair? Just a minute. (*calls over to* GRESHAM) Professor Gresham?

GRESHAM. Yes?

NED. (*into the phone*) He's here all right. Well, I'm just going off duty, Mrs. Wilson. You want to talk to him? (*calls to* GRESHAM *again*) There's a Mrs. Wilson wants to talk to you, Professor.

GRESHAM. (*gets up*) Always fussing after me. Well, I don't want to talk to her. Tell her that. (*He goes off through the exit to the rest rooms.*)

NED. (*to* GRESHAM *as he exits*) Whatever you say. (*into the phone*) Sorry, Mrs. Wilson, he's . . . (*He hesitates.*) . . . not available right now. Well, yes he's here, but he just stepped into the rest room. OK. You want me to give him a message? OK. OK. OK. (MRS. WILSON *apparently goes on and on, but finally* NED *hangs up and turns to* CHRIS.) At least now we know who he is.

CHRIS. (*who has taken his place behind the counter*) What was that all about?

NED. She's worried about him. She thinks he should come home. She thinks it wasn't very nice not to show up for lunch when she'd gone to all the trouble to make sauerbraten. She thinks he's thoughtless to have come down here without telling her. She thinks . . .

CHRIS. (*with a laugh*) You going to give him the message?

NED. She can give it to him herself. Women! (*nods toward the rest room exit*) Like he said, "always fussing." As far I'm concerned the old guy can stay here until midnight.

CHRIS. *I'll* tell him that. Anything I should know about before you leave?

NED. Nothing too important. A batch of petitions came in to reinstate service between here and Lockerbee.

CHRIS. Lockerbee? Way up north?

NED. Yeah. If you get any more just add them to the stack there on the desk. Every few years somebody brings the issue up, but nothing ever comes of it.

CHRIS. I don't remember there being a bus to Lockerbee.

NED. Long before your time, kid. Over thirty years ago.

Even before I transferred here. Anyhow it's a lost cause. The boss told me the company's never going to run a bus up there again. He said it was a jinxed route. One breakdown after another. And finally I guess there was a bad accident. That was the last run. (*He indicates* GRESHAM, *who has wandered back to his place on the bench.*) He's apparently an old-timer here. Could probably tell you all about it. (*He changes the subject and heads for the left exit.*) OK. I guess that's it. See you tomorrow. Be sure everything's locked up tight after the last bus gets in.

CHRIS. Don't worry. I'll take care of it. (*After* NED BARRETT *leaves*, CHRIS *calls over to* GRESHAM.) How's about it, Pops? If you aren't going anywhere, you must be meeting somebody. Right? Somebody special?

GRESHAM. (*The perplexed expression comes over his face again and he rubs his forehead.*) Yes. Yes . . . I am meeting someone. (*There is the sound of the power brakes of a bus offstage right and* CHRIS *looks in that direction.*)

CHRIS. If it's the 4:10 from Millbrook you're waiting for, it just pulled in.

> (*There is offstage activity and bus passengers file into the station.* GRESHAM *gets up and looks anxiously over the crowd. He is jostled a bit but does not seem to be aware of it. Finally when it is ap-*

parent that everyone is off the bus he shakes his head, goes back to the bench, and opens the schedule folder again. CHRIS, *in the meantime, becomes busy with questions from the people who push up to the counter. This is all simultaneous action and when it is over,* CHRIS *sees that* GRESHAM *is still present.*)

CHRIS. Not the one, eh? Don't worry. We'll find a bus for you to meet.

(*At that moment a* YOUNG WOMAN, *wearing warm but shabby clothing, enters from the left. She carries a large box, gift wrapped and tied with bright ribbon, and she keeps looking behind her. Nervously she moves into the center of the station and looks around expectantly.*)

CHRIS. Can I help you, ma'am?

YOUNG WOMAN. (*immediately on the defensive*) I don't need any help. Do I look like I need help?

CHRIS. Just asked, lady, just asked.

YOUNG WOMAN. I'm here to meet a bus, that's all. This is a bus station. I would think you would know that I had come to meet a bus.

CHRIS. Don't get uptight, lady. Just forget it.

(*A man comes in from the street and goes to the counter.* CHRIS *is occupied with business as the* YOUNG WOMAN *crosses to the exit at right and looks out. Then she walks hesitantly to the bench where* GRESHAM *sits.*)

YOUNG WOMAN. (*to* GRESHAM) You would think that man could see I was meeting someone. You would know that, wouldn't you?

GRESHAM. Oh, I suppose so. But perhaps he thought you needed information. You don't have any luggage, but that is no criterion. You could be going someplace.

YOUNG WOMAN. Oh, no, I'm not going anyplace. I doubt whether I could get away.

GRESHAM. (*with a sigh*) I think it would be fine to be too busy to get away for a holiday. I'm not actively engaged in anything anymore. Retired, you see. Of course, I do lecture now and then at the college, but I'm quite sure they request it just to be kind.

YOUNG WOMAN. Some people aren't kind.

GRESHAM. And others are too kind, young lady. Mrs. Wilson, for example. She fusses so. But I guess she means well. She does take good care of me.

YOUNG WOMAN. I don't like to be taken care of. (*She*

changes the subject abruptly.) No, I'm not going any-place. I'm not going *any*place.

GRESHAM. Yes, you said that. You said you were meeting someone.

YOUNG WOMAN. (*brightens up*) Oh, yes. My girl. She's coming for the holidays. It seems like such a long time since I've seen her.

GRESHAM. Away at boarding school? Can't be college. You're too young for that.

YOUNG WOMAN. Oh, no, she's not in college. She's just a little girl. I've brought a present for her.

GRESHAM. An enormous package to be carrying around. Almost as big as you are, young lady. Why didn't you just wait and give it to her at home?

YOUNG WOMAN. (*looks around furtively and then leans over to speak confidentially to him*) I wanted to be sure she got it. She might not be able to come home with me.

GRESHAM. I don't understand.

YOUNG WOMAN. (*Ignoring the question in his words, she speaks with a spirited voice again.*) Besides, she wouldn't want to wait. Would you like to see the pres-ent?

GRESHAM. You have it wrapped to beautifully. Are you sure you want to open it?

YOUNG WOMAN. I don't mind. I can do it up again. I'm good at wrapping boxes and tying bows. You'll see. I do most of the presents at Christmastime. (*Carefully, she unwraps the package and takes out a large stuffed animal toy.*)

GRESHAM. That is a fine present. Your girl is certain to like it. My Gene was always fond of stuffed animals.

YOUNG WOMAN. (*with delight*) You have a little girl too!

GRESHAM. (*laughs*) I'm afraid not. No, Gene is Eugene, and he's no longer little either. Grown up and on his own. Doesn't live with me. I'm glad of that. He fusses about things too. Almost as much as Mrs. Wilson.

YOUNG WOMAN. I forgot to ask. Are you going away?

GRESHAM. No. I'm not going away either, even though I do have sufficient time for travel.

YOUNG WOMAN. Then *you're* meeting somebody?

GRESHAM. (*rubs his forehead and eyes in the gesture of uncertainty*) Yes . . . That's right . . . I am. (*pauses*) I am.

YOUNG WOMAN. Sometimes I think meeting somebody is

better than going away, don't you? What bus are you waiting for?

GRESHAM. (*leans toward her and speaks in a low tone*) Well, you see it is rather embarrassing, young lady, because I don't know what bus. That's why I had to come down early this morning and wait. It may appear foolish, but I didn't want to miss it.

YOUNG WOMAN. I certainly don't blame you for that.

GRESHAM. Mrs. Wilson would, I'm afraid . . . think me foolish that is.

YOUNG WOMAN. Is it your wife you're meeting, Mr. Wilson?

GRESHAM. (*startled*) My wife's dead. Esther's been dead a long time now. A long time.

YOUNG WOMAN. That's too bad. Poor Mrs. Wilson.

GRESHAM. You've got it mixed up, young lady. Mrs. Wilson is my housekeeper. And indeed "keeper" is the proper word.

YOUNG WOMAN. (*Reacts to the word "keeper" and looks about as though expecting someone to come in through the doors to the street. When she speaks again it is with composure.*) As long as there's someone to meet. (*with fresh brightness*) Wouldn't it be nice if my little girl and your . . . whoever it is . . . would be on the same bus?

GRESHAM. That would be quite a coincidence.

YOUNG WOMAN. Wouldn't it be real nice if they shared the same seat? Maybe they are good friends already. Would you like that? Is your . . . does your friend like children?

GRESHAM. That's the other embarrassing circumstance, young lady. I don't know who it is I'm to meet. That must sound very strange. But this entire day has been somewhat strange. Several things have been confusing to me. You see I received this letter, and when I went to check it again, I couldn't find it. Mislaid it I suppose. Dreadful to have the years overtake you so that you mislay things. Always needing someone to remind you.

YOUNG WOMAN. It's the other way with me. I'm the one who remembered about my little girl coming today. I know very well who it is I am to meet.

GRESHAM. (*Following his own train of thought, he does not respond to the young woman's remark.*) Sometimes I think Mrs. Wilson threw that letter away. Deliberately. She could see I was excited about it. (*directs his words to the* YOUNG WOMAN *again*) She says I shouldn't get excited. I have this tricky heart, you see, and Mrs. Wilson and Gene both keep fussing at me not to get keyed up about things.

YOUNG WOMAN. I think a person has every right to get excited when you're expecting someone. I'm excited. But then I don't have a tricky heart. Maybe if you think very hard, you'll remember what bus it is. I'll bet it's the same one my little girl is on. And I'll bet they're just sitting there together talking about the two of us.

GRESHAM. If I could only remember who it is.

YOUNG WOMAN. Whoever it is, I'm sure they're good friends by now. You'll have to come over and have some Christmas cookies and punch with us. (*hesitates and becomes somber and uncertain*) That is if they do truly let her stay.

GRESHAM. They?

YOUNG WOMAN. Where I live. (*leans over to confide in him once more*) I don't think they even wanted me to come to meet her.

GRESHAM. That's incredible, young lady. Why shouldn't you meet her. And as the child's mother you certainly have a right to have her with you, especially at Christmas.

YOUNG WOMAN. (*with a kind of surprise*) That's true, isn't it? Yes. Why shouldn't I meet her. Why shouldn't she come home with me.

(*During the dialogue between* GRESHAM *and the* YOUNG WOMAN, CHRIS *has been busy with customers or his term paper or both and has looked up occasionally but with no particular interest. He looks up again but remains behind the counter when*

MRS. HOFFMAN, *a matronly looking woman, enters from the left. She wears a heavy coat which is in the current style but not particularly fashionable, and with a businesslike air of authority she comes directly to the* YOUNG WOMAN.)

MRS. HOFFMAN. Dolores. (*with a sigh*) I was sure you'd be here. Come along now. It's getting late.

YOUNG WOMAN. (*to* GRESHAM) I said that didn't I? Didn't I tell you they don't want me to meet her?

GRESHAM. (*gets to his feet and addresses* MRS. HOFFMAN) Look now, this young woman is meeting her little girl. Why do you come here and . . .

MRS. HOFFMAN. (*brusquely*) It's all right, Grandpa. We'll take care of her.

YOUNG WOMAN. But he said the truth. Mr. Wilson said the truth. I'm meeting my little girl. She's coming on the bus with Mr. Wilson's friend.

MRS. HOFFMAN. (*gently*) I understand, Dolores, but things don't always work out the way we plan them. You'll have to come home now.

GRESHAM. Now I'm not so sure about that. Who's going to be here when the child gets off the bus? A little girl like that can't get off a bus all alone and no one to meet her.

MRS. HOFFMAN. (*crosses to* GRESHAM, *lowers her voice slightly, and speaks with impatience*) Not that it's any of your business, Grandpa, but there isn't any little girl. Dolores doesn't have a little girl. She never did have a little girl.

(CHRIS *perks up at these statements from* MRS. HOFFMAN *and becomes attentive.*)

GRESHAM. That seems to be a presumptuous statement. I don't understand. The young lady says . . .

MRS. HOFFMAN. (*irritated*) I haven't time to discuss this with you, sir. (*to the* YOUNG WOMAN *with the gentler tone*) Let's get back to Briarwood now, honey, and have a nice dinner. (*She pulls her to her feet and starts to walk toward the left exit.*)

CHRIS. (*who has come from behind the counter, meets* MRS. HOFFMAN *at center stage*) Briarwood? You're from Briarwood?

GRESHAM. (*The reality seems to begin to reach him, but his voice is full of question.*) Briarwood?

CHRIS. (*to* MRS. HOFFMAN) Of course. I recognize you now. Our Psych class visited Briarwood last month. Mrs. Hoffman, isn't it?

MRS. HOFFMAN. That's right, young man. I'm Mrs. Hoffman. And now that the amenities are taken care of, I'll get Dolores home. (*She takes the young woman's arm and speaks to her softly but with a firmness.*) You upset us all when you leave, Dolores, I must confess it makes me cross with you.

CHRIS. (*puts his hand out to hold them back*) I'd like to talk to her, if I may?

MRS. HOFFMAN. There really isn't time for chitchat.

CHRIS. I think we should make time, Mrs. Hoffman. You know I'm right in the middle of a term paper, and that's just what it's about—the need for taking time in our institutions. I'm going to work in your field someday.

MRS. HOFFMAN. Commendable, young man, and get in it quickly. We're very shorthanded. Dolores, here, runs away almost every other day, usually to the bus station. I'd have been down for her sooner, incidentally, except that there was no time.

CHRIS. (*to* MRS. HOFFMAN) A minute can't hurt. (*He turns to the* YOUNG WOMAN *who has been cuddling the stuffed animal and pouting.*) I talked to you at Briarwood too. Do you remember? I'm sorry I didn't know who you were before.

GRESHAM. (*in bewilderment*) This has indeed been a very strange day.

MRS. HOFFMAN. (*Turns to him, suddenly aware of the*

confusion in his voice. She looks at him more closely.)
Say, aren't you John Gresham, Professor Gresham? Yes!
Well, Professor, you should know about Dolores, you of
all people. She was on that bus from Lockerbee with
your wife. That last bus from Lockerbee. She was just
a child then, of course. There were only six passengers
on that bus, thank God, but nonetheless Dolores was the
only survivor.

GRESHAM. (*almost to himself*) Lockerbee. Lockerbee.

MRS. HOFFMAN. I'm not sure she was the lucky one either,
though you might not have seen it that way. Her parents were with her. Both killed. She was left all alone.
We've had her at Briarwood now for almost thirty years.
(*She sighs and turns back to* DOLORES, *but as though
she no longer has the energy to protest she waits for*
CHRIS *to finish talking to the* YOUNG WOMAN.)

CHRIS. I saw the present you unwrapped. I used to collect
stuffed animals. Let me see it. (*He reaches out for the
animal and* DOLORES *pulls back from him.*)

YOUNG WOMAN. You can't have it. It's for my little girl.
(*Then her face puckers up and she looks about to cry.*)
And I didn't get the box done up again.

MRS. HOFFMAN. (*breaks into the conversation*) You can
do that after dinner, Dolores. I'll get fresh paper and
ribbon and you can start all over again. Make it even
prettier than before. (*She tries to steer her toward the*

left exit but the YOUNG WOMAN *stands firm and refuses to move.*)

YOUNG WOMAN. But it will be too late. I'm going to miss her. (*She crosses to* GRESHAM *and thrusts the toy into his arms.*) Here, you give it to her. Tell her I'm sorry it isn't wrapped. I do tie such pretty bows. And tell your friend hello. Maybe you *will* come for cookies.

MRS. HOFFMAN. (*eager to be off*) Certainly they can come for cookies, dear.

CHRIS. (*still hanging on to the opportunity to talk to the* YOUNG WOMAN) I'd like to come too. Could I come?

YOUNG WOMAN. (*hesitates*) I guess you could. If you don't ask to help me. (*She turns and as though a burden is off her shoulders she holds her hand out to* MRS. HOFFMAN *and speaks in a child's voice and with a child's enthusiasm.*) Are we going to have ice cream for dinner?

(MRS. HOFFMAN *and the* YOUNG WOMAN *exit left.* CHRIS *watches them through the door as* GRESHAM *stands in a kind of trance.*)

GRESHAM. Lockerbee . . . Lockerbee. (*He goes to the far end of the right center bench where he was when the curtain opened and sits down, still clutching the toy.*)

CHRIS. (*who has not been paying any attention to* GRESHAM, *now turns to him*) Well, I sure flunked that one. I saw that that woman was acting weird. I should have recognized the pattern. Did you know she was . . . Did you know . . . (*He sees that there is something wrong with* GRESHAM *who sits straight and rigid and with a glassy stare.*) Say, are you all right?

GRESHAM. (*in an odd, expressionless voice*) I have remembered the bus, young man. It is the one from Lockerbee.

CHRIS. What?

(*At this moment* EUGENE GRESHAM *who is in his late thirties, well dressed, obviously a business or professional man, enters from the left and hurries to his father.*)

EUGENE. Look, Dad, Mrs. Wilson called me at the office. She said you didn't come home for lunch, and she was worried about you. She didn't dream you'd come to the bus station, but she talked to Doc Simpson and he said he was sure he saw you head in here. (*He sees there is something amiss.*) Dad!

GRESHAM. It's all right, Gene. I've come to meet the Lockerbee bus.

CHRIS. (*to* EUGENE) He just told me that, mister, and I guess you know there isn't one.

EUGENE. (*ignores* CHRIS) Dad! (*He shakes his arm.*) Mrs. Wilson says you've been rummaging through all those old letters too. That's not good. It's been thirty years ago since ma was killed. No use to bring back all the pain.

GRESHAM. (*in a monotone*) The Lockerbee bus. That's it. The Lockerbee bus. (*He collapses against his son's shoulder, still holding the toy animal.*)

EUGENE. Dad! Dad! (*to* CHRIS) Call an ambulance! And the hospital!

> (CHRIS *goes to the counter and gets on the phone. There are a few people in the station and they crowd around offering to help and adding to the hubbub.*)

EUGENE. Hang on, Dad . . . hang on . . .

> (*There is a slow curtain which falls only part way to the floor to indicate it is not the end of the play. There is the sound of sirens and in a moment or two the curtain rises again. The lights are dimmed.* EUGENE, CHRIS, *and all the people who were on the stage are frozen, immobile.*)

VOICE FROM OFFSTAGE RIGHT. Look alive, you fellows in there. The bus is here from Lockerbee. End of the line, folks. Everybody off.

> (GRESHAM *stirs and then stands, responding to the voice. He watches as five people come through the right entrance. A young couple in their late twen-*

ties. Two elderly women. Finally a woman about thirty-five. They are all dressed in the clothes of thirty years before. When GRESHAM *sees the last woman, who is* ESTHER, *he starts to move slowly toward her. He checks himself, looks down at the stuffed toy in his arms, puts the animal down, pushing it into the far right corner of the bench. Then he goes to meet his wife.*)

GRESHAM. (*greeting* ESTHER *with great affection*) Esther! Esther! How we have missed you.

(*The first four passengers drift past them and exit left.*)

ESTHER. John, it's only been two weeks.

GRESHAM. Seems longer. That's for sure. How was the trip?

ESTHER. The roads were icy, treacherous, and . . .

GRESHAM. I was afraid they would be. How is your mother? Is she going to be all right?

ESTHER. It'll be touch and go for awhile yet, but she was better when I left. She was certainly happy to have me come, John, and to stay as long as I did during the busy Christmas season. Did you get my letter?

GRESHAM. Yes. Yes, I got your letter. I met the bus, didn't I?

ESTHER. Have you and Gene been all right?

GRESHAM. Fine. We've been fine. I don't make a good mother though. Missed you.

ESTHER. Well, I'm home again. And John, there was the sweetest little girl on the bus. She was with her parents, but she came and sat beside me when the snow started to fly. We had such a good visit. We should have a daughter someday, John. (*She looks around.*) I did want you to meet her, but you know when we went to get off the bus I couldn't find her. (*with concern*) It was strange, John, I couldn't find her.

GRESHAM. I'm sure she's all right. Certainly not your responsibility. And if her parents were with her. Come along home, Esther. We've got the tree to decorate and Gene wants to make popcorn strings . . . (*They exit left.*)

> (*The stage is quiet. The actors are still frozen. Then a little girl about five enters from the right. She is dressed in present-day clothing and is obviously frightened. She looks around the station, stands for a moment at center stage. When she sees the stuffed animal she makes a move toward it, but as she reaches for the toy an expression of great sadness comes over her face. Her outstretched arms drop to her sides. She sits down at the other end of the bench, looks longingly at the animal, and sobs as the curtain falls.*)

PRODUCTION NOTES

The Last Bus from Lockerbee takes place in December, and it is cold. This is indicated by the clothing called for. Gresham's overcoat. The warm jackets and caps of the ticket agents. The winter wraps of the Young Woman and Mrs. Hoffman. The dress is modern day except for the five Lockerbee bus passengers. The script is clear on this point.

Gresham is described as having white hair and with a white flower in his buttonhole. These details can be changed. At least some of the travelers would have luggage and would carry Christmas packages. The stuffed animal can be whatever is available as long as it is large, and the box should be wrapped in colorful holiday paper and tied with ribbon.

Since it is the Christmas season, perhaps a decorated tree could stand in the corner between the doors to the street and the ticket counter.

The number of passengers needed for atmosphere and for the necessary action is up to the director. People specifically mentioned are the man who comes in from the street to distract Chris, the four passengers who get off the Lockerbee bus, and the four or five who are in the station when Gresham collapses. Some of the actors might play double roles.

If it is feasible, Mrs. Wilson's telephone voice could be heard, loud but with the words indistinct. Otherwise, Ned might hold the phone away from his ear to emphasize the fact that her voice is piercing.

If a printed program is provided, it might be better to

leave off the names of Esther and the little girl. It is not imperative that the audience be kept in doubt about who is arriving and on what bus, but why give everything away before the curtain goes up.